Deadly Trail

Marilyn Meredith

Hard Shell Word Factory

To Jeanette Southworth
who created my interest in female deputies and their unique problems.

© 2001 Marilyn Meredith
ISBN: 0-7599-0461-8
Trade Paperback
First printing December 2001

eBook ISBN: 0-7599-0370-0
Published November 2001

Hard Shell Word Factory
PO Box 161
Amherst Jct. WI 54407
books@hardshell.com
http://www.hardshell.com
Cover art © 2001 Mary Z. Wolf
All electronic rights reserved.

Chapter 1

THE MUSCULAR, bronze-skinned Yanduchi Indian plunged his Buck knife deep into the sidewall of one of the big tires of the truck fully loaded with newly-cut logs just as Deputy Tempe Crabtree drove her official white Blazer down the rough track. She didn't have to see his face, she recognized him by his build and waist long black braids—Nick Two John.

If it hadn't been for the group of angry loggers, their blocked equipment, and the belligerent demonstrators, the scene might have been idyllic. Lofty cedars and fir trees interspersed with an occasional Sequoia, grew so close together their foliage nearly blocked out the sun. Enormous ferns covered the floor of the forest.

Tempe jammed the brake pedal to the floor and leaped from her vehicle, but not soon enough to prevent Two John from yanking the knife downward and ruining the tire. Before she could reach him, a tall, skinny logger threw down his cigarette and stomped toward Two John. "What the hell's wrong with you, man? You can't get away with that!"

He swung at Two John. The Indian blocked the blow with the arm that held the knife. "Back off, buddy," he growled. "I don't want to hurt you."

With her hand on her baton, Tempe strode toward the grappling men. "Throw down your knife, Nick! Step away from each other. Now!"

"Did you see what he did, deputy?" the logger whined.

"How could I miss it? You're under arrest, Nick. You have the right to remain silent..." She recited the rest of his rights while Two John compliantly put his wrists together behind his back, awaiting handcuffs. He was only a few inches taller than her own five-foot eight.

When she'd finished, he said, "You ought to be ashamed of yourself, Crabtree."

Tempe laughed. "Because I arrested you? I'm only doing my job."

"No, that's not what I meant. You ought be demonstrating right along with me. Doesn't your Yanduchi ancestry mean anything to you?"

"Obviously not what you think it ought to." Tempe led him to the Blazer.

"Didn't your Grandma teach you anything about what it means to be a Native American?" Nick asked.

She opened the door. "I was only eleven when Mama Lena died." When Tempe thought of her grandmother, she remembered herself as a little girl sitting on the comfortable lap with her head against the cushioning bosom, gazing up into the wrinkled brown face and twinkling dark eyes. She remembered her grandma brushing out her long graying hair and braiding it, intertwining colorful beaded ribbons. The memories made Tempe smile and feel sad at the same time. She had loved her grandmother very much.

With Two John locked inside the Blazer, Tempe turned to face the rest of the Save-the-Forest demonstrators who looked out of place in the usually peaceful surroundings. They shouted unintelligible slogans while crowding around her in a threatening manner. Logging in the national forest in the southern Sierra had been a controversial issue for a long time. Tempe had never been drawn into the dispute before. As resident deputy of Bear Creek, she spent her time enforcing the law in and around the small foothill community. But today, when the dispatcher put out the call she had been the nearest to the trouble.

"Quiet down," Tempe said. "Your permit is for a peaceful demonstration. You don't want to join Two John in the jail down in Dennison, do you?"

The voices lowered to a rumble, but the small group continued to press nearer. If there were a problem she couldn't expect much help from the loggers, she'd handed out too many speeding tickets to them. Pulling herself into the driver's seat of the Blazer, she radioed to the substation requesting back-up. A highway patrolman came on to report he was only a few minutes away and would come and take over so she could transport her prisoner.

One overweight woman wearing a sweatshirt and baggy jeans, sandals on dirty feet, and Indian jewelry around her neck, approached Tempe. "You ought to be arresting the loggers, not any of us," she shouted, spraying Tempe with spit. A faint odor of stale perfume and perspiration emanated from her.

"Excuse me, ma'am, but I saw Two John ruin that truck's tire. The loggers haven't broken the law," Tempe said, hoping the highway patrolman would come before the situation exploded. "Like you, they have permission to be working here."

The woman's round face turned red. "The hell you say, the loggers are destroying the forest!"

Tempe glanced around. Though she could see a few stumps of trees that had been cut, the forest still seemed pretty much intact, but she wasn't about to get into an argument with the woman. "Listen, ma'am. You do have a permit for this demonstration, but it doesn't give you the right to interfere with the logging operation. I suggest you direct your energies to moving the obstacles you've put across the road blocking the equipment."

"Hah! No way!" the woman said, and whirled around, her large buttocks wiggling as she rejoined her friends. They began their shouting again.

Tempe shook her head. She couldn't understand their words and didn't want to. She looked over the motley group. The men seemed to be in the late thirties to early fifties, long haired with mustaches and beards. They didn't look much different from the loggers who leaned against their trucks and equipment, disgust and frustration on their faces. The women demonstrators ranged in age from late twenties to sixties, most of them had lots of hair, a few had tamed theirs with bright scarves. Some wore full skirts, blouses, open vests, and what looked like homemade necklaces. No one seemed familiar. Except for Two John, they must have all been imported for the event.

She heard a vehicle arrive, and gratefully watched a black-and-white highway patrol car park near hers. A large imposing figure stepped from the vehicle, and Tempe smiled as she watched the demonstrators visibly shrink away.

Despite the authority displayed by her own crisp, khaki uniform, Tempe had to admit being a big, male law enforcement officer certainly had its advantages.

"Sure glad you're here, Stevens," Tempe said.

"Giving you a bad time, Crabtree?" The officer peered through mirrored sun glasses past Tempe at the gathering.

"Nothing serious, but I'm sure their behavior will improve now that you're here."

"Who you got there?" the officer asked with a nod of his head toward the Blazer.

"A local by the name of Two John. Caught him slashing the tire of that lumber truck."

"Oh, yes. I'm well acquainted with Nick Two John. Arrested him a couple of times for drunk driving. Ornery as hell when he's drinking."

Tempe expected him to make some crack about Indians not being able to handle liquor but he didn't. He probably held back because of her own Native American heritage. "Nick quit drinking a while back."

"Glad to hear it. You can go ahead and take him in. I'll watch over this so-called peaceful demonstration until more deputies arrive."

"Thanks."

As Tempe walked back to the Blazer, Stevens tucked his thumbs into his belt, spread his legs, and said, "Haven't any of you people got anything more productive to do with your time than interfere with hardworking citizens?"

As soon as she fastened her seat belt and started the engine, Nick said, "Didn't you ever have any curiosity about your Native American heritage?"

Tempe maneuvered the Blazer down the narrow, winding dirt track. What came back to Tempe was the way she had been teased at school because of her Indian blood made obvious by her straight black hair, her copper skin color, and prominent cheek bones. Though surprisingly blue, her eyes were the same almond shape as her grandmother's. She'd been called "half breed" and "squaw" by some of the kids. During her growing up years, she'd found little reason for pride in her ancestry.

"If you want the truth, Nick, I felt ashamed of my Indian blood when I was growing up...and that made me feel bad because it made me think I didn't respect my grandmother's memory. But now, to be perfectly honest, I don't even think about it anymore."

"You're missing out on an important part of your life, Crabtree."

"Maybe so but it isn't anything I've noticed."

"I used to be like that back in my drinking days. It wasn't until I nearly killed myself driving off that cliff that I realized how I was wasting my life."

Tempe remembered the accident that occurred after Nick had spent the evening drinking in a local bar. Following a long stay in the hospital, he'd gotten a job at the Bear Creek Inn.

Tempe glanced in the rear view mirror. Nick Two-John's eyes stared at her with what looked like pity. He was handsome and had the reputation of being a ladies' man. He'd been a year or two behind her in school, so she hadn't really known him until she'd moved back to Bear Creek after her husband, a highway patrolman, was killed in the line of duty. When no one could remember her married name, Tempe had taken back her maiden name of Crabtree.

"How's your job?" Tempe asked.

"Good. Been there almost two years now."

Tempe drove out onto the highway that led down to the small community where she made her home with her sixteen year-old son, Blair. She would be driving on through Bear Creek and down into Dennison to book Two John into the small jail at the substation.

Right before they reached the two block stretch of highway that made up the business portion of Bear Creek, they passed the Inn. Once a stage coach stop, the sprawling log building had been added onto and turned into a hotel during the thirties. Remodeled again in the seventies, it had become a popular restaurant for people driving up the twenty miles from Dennison and even farther. Under the management of the latest owners, it had undergone even more changes.

"Stop!" Nick shouted.

"Sorry," Tempe said. "Can't do that."

"Hey, just let me tell Claudia what's going on so she can spring me."

"You'll have the opportunity to make a call after you've been booked. Tell her then."

"C'mon, Crabtree. Doesn't our kindred blood mean anything to you?" His voice had softened.

"Nope."

"You're one hard bitch."

"Just doing my job." She glanced in her rear view mirror once again.

Nick had turned in his seat to stare back at the Inn. "You may look like you've got Yanduchi blood, but it must be too diluted by the white part to do you any damn good."

"Sorry I'm such a disappointment to you, Nick," Tempe said lightly, Nick's opinion of her and her profession meant nothing. She loved her job as resident deputy of Bear Creek despite some of its drawbacks. Having to arrest a fellow resident was one of them.

"Damn, I should have told Claudia what I was going to be doing today, then my arrest wouldn't come as such a shock to her."

Tempe knew Nick was thinking out loud. "You should have considered how your actions might affect your job before you slashed that tire."

Nick chuckled. "I don't have to worry about my job. Claudia and I are pretty tight."

So, the rumors about Two John and his employer, Claudia Donato were true. "Maybe Mr. Donato won't be as generous."

"Andre Donato is too busy with his own affairs to even suspect anything about me and Claudia." Nick winked at her reflection in the mirror.

"I see," Tempe said, but wondered what kind of affairs Nick was referring to—business, pleasure, or both. Andre and Claudia Donato had made significant improvements since they purchased the Inn. The menu had become more sophisticated without losing any of the food's quality, they hired entertainment for the weekend crowd, and the couple were both highly visible in their establishment and the community.

There had been other changes too, changes that involved Nick Two John. Nick had been hired to create a nature trail to attract more visitors and to occupy hotel guests during
the day time. The attraction necessitated his staying on to keep it up and to act as a guide, giving him a full time job—and obviously a bit more. Tempe didn't care to know the details about the latter.

"Tell me about your nature trail. I've been trying to get Blair to come with me to take it in."

"Blair? Oh, sure, he's your kid. Be good for both of you. Make you aware of a bit of your heritage...you certainly could use some educating along those lines."

"Once you're out of jail, we'll do that. I bet Blair would get a kick out of it."

"Might bring along that preacher boyfriend of yours too. Probably do him some good."

Tempe felt her face flush. She didn't look up in the
mirror. Keeping her voice steady, she said, "Yes, I'm sure you're right, Hutch would enjoy it. He is interested in that sort of thing."

"I take a bunch out nearly every afternoon, usually around two."

Tempe drove the remainder of the way in silence. When she pulled into the parking lot of the sheriff's substation and started to get out of the Blazer, Nick leaned forward.

"Hold on, Crabtree," he said, a sense of urgency in his voice. "Listen to me for a minute."

"There's nothing you can possibly say that's going to change things, Two John. I've arrested you, and now I'm taking you inside to be booked." She opened the back door to let him out.

He stuck one foot and his head out, staring up at her.

"Reconsider. There's lots of stuff going on in Bear Creek that you don't know about. Things that are going to affect a bunch of folks. Turn me loose and I'll let you in on some startling information."

"Sorry, Two John. Get out of the car."

He climbed out slowly. She took hold of his arm and guided him toward the stairs that led to the back door of the plain, boxy building. His face sullen, his black eyes flashed with anger. "You're going to remember that I gave you the opportunity to prevent what's about to happen in Bear Creek. You're going to be real, real sorry you didn't listen."

Chapter 2

"I DON'T KNOW why I have to tag along," Blair, Tempe's sixteen-year-old son, said. "What a boring way to spend a day off from school." The teachers at Dennison High were having an in-service, giving the students a holiday.

True to his word, Nick Two John was bailed out of jail by his boss, Claudia Donato. As Tempe had promised him, on her first day off she was headed for Bear Creek Inn to go on Nick's nature walk. But first she planned to pick up her fiance, Hutch, and take him along.

"I think it's an excellent use of your time off." Tempe turned the Blazer onto the road leading to Hutch's ranch. "You can learn some facts about your Indian heritage. Something I haven't done and probably should have."

With his six-foot frame scrunched down in the seat beside her, Blair made an unpleasant noise. He swiped at a lock of his light, cornsilk hair. It was cut in the latest fashion favored by the high school crowd. Except for his blue, almond-shaped eyes, his long, strong-jawed face did not look much like Tempe.

Situated about two miles above town, Hutch's ranch snuggled in a broad valley surrounded by mountains. Tempe drove the Blazer down the winding road to the two-story, gray-and-white house. A huge red barn loomed behind it. Cows grazing in the open pasture turned curious eyes toward the vehicle.

A widower, Hutch lost his wife to cancer several years ago. Even though they hadn't dwelled on it, the fact that they both had lost spouses they loved very much had created a deep and instant bond between them.

Tempe parked near the wide veranda-style front porch, and Blair crossed his arms over his chest and scooted even lower in the seat.

"What's the matter now?" Tempe asked.

"As long as we have to do this, why do we have to take the preacher along?"

"Because I thought it would be a pleasant outing for us to do together. After all, Hutch is going to be your step-father. You need to spend some time getting acquainted."

"He's going to be your husband...not my father."

"Here comes Hutch now. Please be nice." Tempe hoped Blair would eventually accept Hutch. Because of her job she couldn't devote as much time to her son as she would have liked. And now, what little time they did have together had to be shared. No doubt Blair was feeling a bit jealous.

Hutch, in worn Levis and cowboy boots and a plaid, short-sleeved shirt that exposed his muscular arms, bounded down the wide steps of the front porch. As usual, his thick, auburn hair looked as though he'd been running his fingers through it.

Tempe nudged her son. "Hop in the back, honey. Let Hutch sit up here with me."

"Oh brother." After rolling his eyes at her, Blair opened the passenger door and climbed out.

Tempe admired Hutch's lean but well-muscled physique as he extended his hand toward Blair. "How's it going?"

Blair mumbled something that might have been, "Okay." He ignored the offered gesture.

Amusement sparkled in Hutch's gray eyes as he climbed in next to Tempe. After kissing her, he said, "I'm really looking forward to this."

From the back came, "Glad someone is."

Hutch turned toward Blair. "You like horses? Come on over some time and we'll go riding."

"Didn't know you were a cowboy too."

"I'm not. The cattle don't belong to me, I lease out the pasture. But I do own a couple of nice horses and there are some good trails on the ranch. Like to have you ride with me sometime."

"Naw, I don't really like horses much," Blair said.

Hutch lifted an eyebrow in Tempe's direction and winked. She reached over and patted his hand to let him know she appreciated his attempt to make friends with Blair. That was one of many traits that attracted Tempe to Hutch. He wasn't afraid to show compassion, unlike the men she came in contact with on the job, never displaying emotion of any kind.

Hutch grinned, displaying his deeply dimpled cheeks. "I've been meaning to take this tour but never seemed to find time. Native American lore has always fascinated me."

"I was telling Blair that it's time he learned something about his heritage."

"No one every believes I've got any Indian blood in me, so I don't see what difference it makes," Blair grumbled.

"That's understandable," Hutch said.

"You look a lot like your dad did when I first met him. But the fact remains, Blair, I am your mother, and you do have Yanduchi blood in your veins. So you might as well learn something about your ancestors."

"Humor her, Blair. You might even find this entertaining," Hutch said

Again Blair rolled his eyes. "I doubt it. I bet you have better things to do too."

"Ministers do get a day off now and then, and I like to spend as much time with your mother as I can."

"You guys ought to be doing something romantic instead of going on a dumb hike," Blair said.

"We're saving the romance for this evening." Hutch grinned again, dimples flashing.

He patted Tempe's hand, and Blair groaned.

She parked in the lot behind the sprawling two-story log structure, and they walked to the starting point of the trail. Blair dragged along behind his mother and the minister.

Besides educating her son and keeping her promise to Two John, she had another reason for taking the time to go on the guided tour. Though she'd judged the Yanduchi's mysterious threat as a desperate attempt to keep his freedom, his words nagged at her. If there was something going on in Bear Creek that she ought to know about, she should investigate. She considered what they were about to do the beginning of that investigation.

Several cars were parked in the area reserved for guests and near what Tempe knew was the outside kitchen door. She recognized the Donatos' cars, Andre's silver Cadillac and Claudia's black Mustang, along with several older vehicles including Two John's tan, battered Ford truck.

"Here's where it begins," Hutch said, pointing out a hand carved and painted sign which read: "INDIAN TRAIL, starting time 2 p.m., wait for guide."

Blair glanced at his watch. "It's five after and no one's here. Let's go."

"Don't be so impatient. Nick will be along any moment, I'm sure."

Blair sighed.

A screened door banged, and Nick Two John strode toward them. His long braids swung against his broad shoulders as he picked up his pace after noticing people waited for him. When he recognized Tempe, just for a moment, a shadow crossed his handsome face. When he reached them, he greeted her without offering his hand.

"I didn't ever expect to see you here." Two John yanked on the bead decorated leather vest he wore over a blue T-shirt. His Levis were shabby and worn, the toes of his boots scuffed. "You look more Yanduchi out of uniform."

"I told you I would, and I always keep my promises." As usual, Tempe had brushed her long black hair into a single braid that instead of coiling and fastening to the back of her head, she let hang down the middle of her back. She had on comfortable jeans and sneakers, and a long sleeved yellow blouse with a blue cardigan tied around her shoulders. "You know Hutch, don't you?" Tempe asked. "And this is my son, Blair."

"Yeah, I've seen both of you around."

"Are we going to be the only ones?" Tempe asked, anxious to get moving.

"Looks that way. It's usually slow during the week unless we have some new guests. But everyone who is registered now has been on the tour already." He glanced toward the inn. "Let's get started."

He led them onto a path which wound through an herb garden. "Every herb used in cooking and for our special teas is grown right here." A touch of pride stole into Nick's voice. Tempe knew he'd planted and tended to the grounds. She recognized the mint, parsley and chives but had no idea what any of the others were.

A heady scent of blooming flowers and a burst of colors confronted them just beyond the herbs. Both sides of the path had been planted with dainty Lily of the Valley framed by baby's breath, every color of rose bush, backed by hedges of jasmine with its bright yellow trumpet blossoms.

Two John halted, and turned to face his audience. Speaking directly to Tempe, he said, "I suppose you think this is merely a pretty garden."

"It is certainly beautiful," she said, not knowing what he meant.

"The cook uses the rose hips to make tea and jam. Our ancestors made medicine from the jasmine's blossoms for whooping cough and asthma. The roots were used for sedatives and painkillers. But you have to be careful when using this because it can be poisonous."

"Really?" Blair's bored expression disappeared, and he stared at the flowers with more interest.

Two John leaned down and broke off one of the Lily of the Valley blooms. "This certainly looks innocent, doesn't it? Like many of the plants we will see today, it has many uses. Made into tea it can ease the pain of gout, and added to wine it will help the old peoples' memory."

He paused, dropped the flower and ground it under the heel of his buckskin boot. "But like so many of the others, along with its healing powers, it is also poisonous."

"I had no idea," Hutch said.

And neither did Tempe. She wondered if this revelation had anything to do with Two John's warning about things going on in Bear Creek that might affect a lot of people.

"You're going to find out plenty you never knew before," Two John said. He whirled on his heel causing his long braids to fly, and the beads on his vest to click.

After leaving the planted garden, they came upon a small meadow. "Look closely, and you'll see many wild flowers. We use the dandelions to make tea and wine.

"In the early mornings and evenings, deer graze here. Use your eyes and look at everything carefully. Even the weeds are useful to the Yanduchi."

Blair poked Tempe and whispered, "What's the matter with this guy, Mom? He acts like he's doing us some big favor or something."

"Don't let it bother you," Tempe murmured. She waited until Nick had gotten quite a ways ahead of them before she added, "He's mad at me because I arrested him the other day."

One corner of Blair's mouth lifted. "Oh yeah? What'd he do?"

"I'll tell you later."

"You'd better. Makes this hike a bit more interesting." Blair strode off on his long legs, easily catching up with Two John.

Blair pointed to a scraggly white mustard plant. "What about this? What's it good for?"

"Mustard plasters and laxatives," Two John said.

"Oh, my goodness," Tempe said. "I remember mustard plasters. My grandmother used to put them on me when I had the flu." The memory of the burning sensation on her tender skin and the acrid smell associated with the strange poultice came back to her.

"And that?" Blair asked, pointing toward an ugly, tall weed.

"It's wormseed. Long ago we used it to get rid of worms in humans."

"Ugh, sorry I asked." Blair made a face.

Hutch stepped close to a thistle. "This one is nothing but a pest."

"That's where you're wrong, Pastor," Two John said.

"The fruit of the thistle is healing to the liver. Tastes pretty good too."

"How about that." Hutch nodded.

Tempe noted the difference between the two men. Two John wasn't much taller than Tempe's five foot eight while Hutch was six foot. Both men were muscular though Hutch was leaner. Two John's hair was blue-black, his eyes dark, his skin bronze, his expression solemn. The breeze ruffled Hutch's auburn hair, interest apparent in his eyes, freckles were scattered across his lightly tanned skin, and despite their guide's prickly manner, a smile played on his lips. He seemed to be enjoying the tour. He reached out and gave Tempe a quick hug around the waist before they moved on.

Two John pointed out a cluster of sweet violet which he said was a cure for skin cancer, the feathery delicate leaves of yarrow which resembled fern with its cream colored heads could be ground into powder to be used on cuts, and Anise cough drops and other medicines. "Here at the Inn we use the Anise leaves in salads, and to flavor some of the baked goods."

"Isn't it kind of dangerous to be cooking with this stuff since so much of it is poisonous?" Blair asked.

"I've been wondering about that too," Tempe said. Though she'd taken the required toxicology class at the Academy, not much time was spent on poisonous plants. She hadn't realized how accessible death could be.

"It would be dangerous for those of you who don't know anything about these plants. But you've got to remember, my people have always taken advantage of everything around for their food and medicine. I grew up knowing about all this...what you can use and how to use it. And I'm the one who trained the cooks." Two John squared his shoulders with pride.

She didn't know much about Two John beyond his conquered alcohol problem and his fierce pride in his heritage. His knowledge about all the available poisons certainly made her more curious about him.

On the other side of the meadow, Two John led them into the forest. He pointed out the different kinds of trees, "That's a yellow pine...there's a wild peach...and just beyond, slippery elm. My people used the bark to make straps for carrying heavy loads. And over there are black oaks. I'm sure that even you know, Tempe, what the acorns were used for."

The man could certainly be irritating. "Of course I do. Acorns were the main food source."

"Very good."

The path led downward toward a stream. On the other side was a clearing with a group of bark huts. "This is the kind of home our ancestors lived in long ago, Crabtree." Deer hides covered the entrances.

"Those houses are little, I couldn't even stand up inside," Blair said.

"My people were much smaller in those days."

"Probably from eating all those poisonous plants and flowers."

Two John ignored Blair's remark. "We need to move along." He marched off ahead of them. "The boss has some errands for me to do before the dinner crowd shows up."

He made a big loop through the forest, identifying other trees along the way as they hiked at a brisk pace. He told them of the many ways the Yanduchi used the leaves, the bark, and the wood.

Because Tempe could see the roof of the Inn she knew they'd made a full circle and nearly reached the end of the trail.

Two John continued to give medicinal purposes and food uses for even more of the plants, weeds, and wild flowers, even the mistletoe dangling from several branches of a white oak. Besides their beneficial uses, many of them were also poisonous.

"Seems like almost everything that can be used for good has a bad side," Blair said.

Hutch added, "Just like people."

"Right, though most white men don't recognize that fact."

"In my business I'm reminded all the time."

Nick looked as though he doubted Hutch but made no further comment. Tempe studied Two John, again wondering if he'd ever consider using his knowledge for harm.

The trail came out on the other side of the herb garden, near the kitchen door. "That's it, folks. Hope it helps you appreciate who you came from, Crabtree and you too, Blair."

Tempe started to thank him but a loud thud and a piercing scream coming from inside the Inn stopped her.

Chapter 3

AS SHE DASHED toward the kitchen door, Tempe's hand instinctively dropped to where her holster would be if she'd been in uniform. Footfalls pounded the pavement behind her and she knew Two John, Hutch, and Blair were in close pursuit.

The scream had died down to short spurts of what sounded like, "No, no! Keep away! Help me! Someone, please!" Tempe had no idea what she'd find when she yanked open the screen door and entered the kitchen.

The huge room contrasted sharply with the rustic outside appearance of the Inn. Obviously, many of the Donatos' refurbishing dollars had been spent on the food preparation area. Stainless steel appliances gleamed in the sunlight that poured through the windows. Copper-bottomed kettles and pots hung from an oval holder suspended from the ceiling.

The screams came from a pretty, teen-aged girl cowering in the corner near the door which led to the walk-in freezer. Her black eyes were huge with fear, her dark brown curly hair had been combed back from her face and covered by a net. A full white apron nearly hid her T-shirt and shorts. She held a broom in front of her like a weapon.

"Lupe! What on earth is all this racket about!"

Tempe recognized Elise Carmony, the Inn's kitchen manager, even though there was something quite different about the middle-aged woman's appearance.

Elise's slightly protruding eyes were emphasized by heavily mascaraed lashes as she watched Tempe and the three men crowding their way inside.

Lupe pointed toward the sink. "A mouse," she gasped. "I saw a mouse. I tried to kill it with the broom, but it got away."

Tempe relaxed, and smiled.

Elise lifted her darkly penciled brows. "For goodness sake, Lupe. You made all that commotion over a little mouse? Set a trap and get back to work." She turned toward Tempe. "And what can I do for you, Deputy Crabtree?"

"Nothing. I heard Lupe too. Just came to see if I could be of assistance."

Hutch stepped toward the still trembling girl. "Don't worry, Lupe, that little mouse won't hurt you."

"Yeah. You probably scared it as much as it scared you," Blair put in.

Lupe noticed him for the first time and grinned. "Oh, hi, Blair. I've always been scared of mice."

"Haven't seen you around school lately."

Her black lashes shadowed her cheeks momentarily. "That's because I dropped out, but it's okay."

"Do you like working here?" Blair asked.

"Yeah, it's great...except for the mouse."

"One of the things you learn to put with living in the mountains," Nick put in.

Elise propped a fist on her plump hip. "I'm afraid I must put a stop to this visiting, as pleasant as it may be, but I have a kitchen to run here. In a few hours customers will be expecting to order dinner and we won't be ready if my help spends the rest of the afternoon standing around chatting."

"Sorry," Tempe said, "we'll get out of your way."

Hutch waved at her and smiled engagingly. "Tempe and I will be here tonight. We're really looking forward to enjoying one of your wonderful dinners."

Elise nodded impatiently.

Two John held the door open. "She's a real bitch at times," he muttered as he followed them out.

When they all reached the parking lot, he added, "Ever since Andre started carrying on with her, she's been acting like she's the boss."

"Elise? What do you mean by carrying on?" Tempe asked.

"He flirts with her all the time. I wouldn't be surprised if she isn't one of his many conquests."

Tempe realized why Elise looked different. She used to be rather frumpy looking, but she'd had her graying hair tinted and styled, and had on make-up which Tempe didn't remember the woman wearing previously. She wondered what Elise's husband, Wilbur, thought about the change.

"How's Lupe doing in her new job?" Hutch asked, in an obvious attempt to change the subject.

"She's a hard worker and ordinarily seems real happy about living up here," Nick said.

Some of the Inn's staff lived in small cabins on the grounds. Because of Blair's friendship with the girl, Tempe knew that Lupe had an abusive step-father. Leaving Dennison and her family had taken a lot of courage.

"Hey, Mom, come on, I want to get home," Blair said.

"Thank you, Nick, for taking us on the hike and sharing all that interesting information," Tempe said, smiling.

"Yes, thanks a lot." Hutch shook Two John's hand.

"Just part of my job. Glad you finally took the time to come out. Nearly everyone in Bear Creek has done it now."

"Mom."

"Okay, okay, Blair, we're going. Maybe we'll see you tonight, Nick."

"Yeah, maybe."

HUTCH HELPED Tempe into her chair and leaned down to whisper in her ear. "You look fantastic this evening."

"Thank you." Tempe smiled at him. She was glad she'd decided to wear her only dressy outfit, a simple turquoise silk dress. She'd loosened her hair from its braid and brushed it out over her shoulders. A touch of blush to her cheekbones and gloss on her lips was all the make-up she ever wore, along with a her favorite perfume it was enough to make her feel wonderfully feminine.

Hutch pulled his chair closer to Tempe and sat down. There were only a few other diners in the Inn, mostly Bear Creek residents, Tempe expected the majority of the patrons would arrive later. A stone fireplace dominated the large dining room, the worn wooden floors gleamed with polish.

Each of the round tables had been covered with a pale blue, floor length linen cloth and decorated with a crystal vase displaying a single white, bell-shaped fragrant Lily-of-the-Valley.

Claudia Donato had greeted them upon their arrival, taken them to their seat and given them a menu before disappearing.

Taking hold of Tempe's hand, Hutch squeezed gently. "I want this to be a very special night for us, Tempe."

Her heart fluttered with anticipation; she suspected Hutch wanted to set a date for their wedding. It seemed each time they seriously discussed getting married, something happened with her job to prevent it. She cared deeply for Hutch. He'd already changed her life, giving her so much more to look forward to each day.

"I've been looking forward to being with you."

Hutch grinned, his dimples deepened and his eyes danced. "Tempe, I love you from the depths of my soul."

"I love you, too, Hutch."

He stared at her for a long while and she knew he wanted to take her into his arms, but instead he released her hand. Reaching up, he caressed her cheek. "You are so beautiful."

"Thank you." Though she'd never thought of herself as beautiful, tonight she felt as if she were.

"Being married to you will be so wonderful."

"I can hardly wait."

"Well. I suppose we ought to look at the menu." He pulled his tortoise-framed glasses from his pocket and slipped them on. He only wore them to read and when he preached his sermons. Tempe smiled at his only vanity.

After glancing at the list of entrees for a moment, he added, "They've made a few additions since we were here last."

As they studied the varied choices, Tempe became aware of voices coming from the direction of the Inn's office. At first, the words weren't understandable, but as they grew louder it was obvious that the Donatos were having an argument.

"Putting up bail for that damn Indian is more than I can overlook," Andre shouted.

"What about you and Elise? And all the others, for that matter."

"None of them meant a rat's ass to me and you know it."

Scowling, Elise Carmony came rushing through the double swinging doors from the kitchen and without looking around, stomped to the door of the office. She knocked sharply and was admitted inside. The angry words stopped.

"Guess Mrs. Carmony let the Donatos know they could be heard all over the dining room," Hutch said.

Elise came out and marched deliberately back into the kitchen. In a few moments, Andre made his appearance. A dignified European of mixed ancestry, he reminded Tempe of a movie star of the forties. He had a full head of silver hair, and his mustache was small and neatly trimmed, unlike the big, bushy ones many of the men in Bear Creek sported. He flipped the white silk scarf he wore over the shoulder of his dark blue lamb's wool blazer as he scanned the dining room. Andre always wore some sort of scarf tied around his neck. Tempe suspected it was to hide his crepey skin. In his hand was a large glass with golden liquid.

He spotted Tempe and Hutch, his thin lips parted in a smile, and he headed toward them.

"Darn." Hutch returned his glasses to his suit pocket. "I think he's coming over."

"I'm afraid you're right," Tempe said. "Hello, Mr. Donato."

"Two of my favorite people. Welcome to Bear Creek Inn," he said with only the hint of an accent, as he pulled out a chair. "Do you mind if I join you for a moment?"

Without waiting for an answer he sat down. He took a deep swallow from his glass. When he set it in front of him, he glanced at the table, and said, "Oh, dear, I didn't realize you haven't anything to drink. Where on earth is Lupe?"

"It's all right," Hutch said, quickly. "We just arrived We haven't even had time to decide what we want."

Andre's deep set eyes glittered from beneath thick, silvery brows. "I have a wonderful idea. Why don't you let me go into the kitchen and order you something special?"

"Don't go to any trouble for us..." Tempe began.

"It won't be any trouble, just something to make your evening memorable." Andre took another deep swallow from his glass. He rubbed his temple and frowned slightly.

"Like me, I know you don't drink alcoholic beverages, Pastor... though for a different reason, I'm sure. But maybe you'd like to try one of our specialty teas, hot or iced like mine."

"No, I think I'll just stick to coffee," Hutch said.

"What about you, Deputy?"

"Sure, why not?" Tempe quickly glanced at the menu. "I'll try the sweet clover tea. Hot, please."

Andre stood and picked up his glass. "Good choice. What I'm drinking is a mixture they brew fresh for me each day. It's a satisfying replacement for the stronger stuff."

The man's skin seemed blotchy, and Tempe wondered if he might be ill.

In his self-confident manner, Andre said, "I can assure you both, you'll be delighted with my choice for your dinner. Enjoy." With glass in hand, he strode toward the kitchen.

When Andre had disappeared, Tempe explained, "Donato is a recovering alcoholic.

"Good for him."

"He doesn't look like he's feeling too well."

"Hope it's not something contagious if he's going to be fixing our food."

Tempe laughed. "I doubt if he'll do anything more than give someone orders. Andre doesn't strike me as the type who spends any time cooking."

"My guess is he doesn't do much physical labor of any kind."

Lupe came through the swinging doors next, carrying a tray with two cups, a coffee carafe and small China teapot. Her big apron and shorts had been exchanged for a neat, pale blue uniform with white lace collar and lace trimmed apron.

When she neared their table, Hutch asked, "Any more trouble with the mouse, Lupe?"

Tears glistened in her eyes. "They caught it in the trap. It was awful." She put their cups in front of them, and the pots on the table. "Would you like me to pour for you?"

"No, we can manage. Thank you," Tempe said.

After she'd gone, Hutch said, "Poor girl was scared to death of that mouse this afternoon and ready to do it in herself with the broom, now she's sad because the mouse is dead."

Tempe poured Hutch's coffee and her own tea. "That's no stranger than Andre pretending like nothing had happened before he joined us at the table."

"People are truly fascinating," Hutch said.

"They sure are." Tempe tasted her tea. It had a pleasant vanilla flavor. "This is good."

Lupe brought their salads which looked more like flower arrangements. "Mr. Donato says if you aren't brave enough to try these, you can have the regular kind."

Hutch stared suspiciously at his. "If you'll tell me what this is, I'll decide whether or not to eat it."

"It's violet and pansy blossoms, dandelion leaves, watercress and spinach." She leaned closer. "Sounds weird, but really, it's pretty good."

"If you're recommending it, then I'll eat it," Tempe said, reaching for her salad fork. Though unusual, the combination of flowers and greens which had been dressed lightly with oil, vinegar and herbs, was quite tasty.

Hutch took a bit longer to take his first bite.

Lupe brought them a sliced small loaf of bread. "You'll really like this. Mrs. Carmony made up the recipe, besides whole grain, it's got cattail pollen in it."

After she'd left again, Hutch said, "I'm beginning to wonder what we're going to have for the entree. Might be something like turtle stew."

"Or rattlesnake steaks."

"Maybe roasted squirrel."

"Could be quail, or pheasant."

"I'll be grateful if it's something that normal."

But they needn't have worried. Except for a strange but tasty vegetable which Lupe explained was nettle shoots, the remainder of the dinner was delicious. Andre had chosen spring lamb which had been cooked with lots of garlic and a hint of rosemary.

"Usually I'm not all that crazy about lamb," Hutch said, "but this is great. However, the best part of this dinner is having you beside me. It's been a long time since I've shared meals with a woman I love."

"I know. And it's been wonderful to have someone to speak my thoughts to."

"That's why I'm anxious for us to be married, so we can have more time to be together."

Tempe smiled. It had also been a long while since anyone shared her bed, and she was eagerly awaiting that part of their marriage too.

They didn't talk much more until they were finished. Hutch pushed his plate away, and turned toward Tempe. "Sweetheart, don't you think it's time we set a date? I want you to be my wife...I've certainly mentioned that often enough."

"There's nothing that would make me happier. I have some vacation coming..."

Elise Carmony burst through the doors of the kitchen. My God, someone come quick! Help, please!"

Chapter 4

THE DOOR OF the office opened and Claudia stepped out, "Elise, for goodness sake. What is going on out here?"

Several years younger than her husband, the sophisticated Claudia Donato's pretty face was marred by her annoyance.

"Come quickly, it's Andre...Mr. Donato. He's having an attack or something," Elise gasped, plucking at the full sleeve of Claudia's ivory blouse.

Claudia pulled away from her distastefully. "What do you mean an attack?"

"He's really sick. Please. Come see for yourself."

Tempe tossed her napkin on the table and stood. "Come on, Hutch, let's see if we can be of some help. I knew he didn't look well."

They found Andre Donato sitting on the floor, leaning at an odd angle against the wall. He no longer held his glass. It was broken beside him, the contents spilled. Vomit stained his scarf and blazer. The kitchen staff hovered nearby with varied expressions, some anxious, others merely curious.

Claudia suppressed a scream with her hand. "My God, what's the matter with him?"

Elise sobbed uncontrollably.

Tempe knelt beside the unconscious Andre. She put her hand on his forehead, it felt cold and clammy. Pressing her fingers against his neck, she felt his pulse—uneven and faint. "Hutch, call 911. This man needs medical help fast."

"Where's the phone?" Hutch asked.

Claudia pointed to one on the wall.

"Can't you do something?" Elise gasped.

"Someone from the fire department will be here soon," Tempe assured her. The station was less than a block from the Inn. It would take much longer time for an ambulance to arrive from Dennison.

Sounding hysterical, Claudia said, "What good is a fireman? Andre needs a doctor. He looks like he's going to die."

Tempe agreed. His face was ashen and his breathing shallow.

Before Tempe could explain that the volunteer firemen were medically trained, Pete Roundtree burst through the swinging doors. Another Yanduchi, Pete, as captain of Bear Creek's Fire Department, was the only paid employee.

"What's going on?" he asked. "I was on my way home and heard the call on my radio. That's Andre Donato, isn't it." He knelt down and pressed his fingers against the stricken man's neck. Pete shook his head.

"He's not breathing." Pete stretched Andre out on the floor, and began CPR. He continued for several minutes, everyone watching in horrified fascination, before two volunteers burst through the door, bringing medical equipment from the fire truck. An oxygen mask was placed over Andre's face, and one of the volunteers, a middle-aged woman named Charlene Goodson, took over the chest compressions.

Elise, with her hands covering her face, sobbed loudly.

Claudia paced the floor. "Where's the ambulance? My husband needs real medical care."

"Don't worry, Mrs. Donato, the firemen know what they are doing," Hutch said.

She frowned. "I know these people. One is a cowboy and the other is a grandmother who owns the hardware store. Andre deserves a real doctor."

"I'll give Dr. McClatchey a call and see if he can come up here." Hutch moved toward the telephone.

"He can't do anything more than what we are," Pete mumbled.

Elise cried even louder.

"Hush, Elise," Claudia scolded. "After all Andre is my husband."

The stricken woman quieted, only the sounds of her sniffling came from behind the corner of the apron she used to mop the tears from her face.

Hutch hung up the phone. "We're in luck. The doctor will be right here."

Dr. McClatchey lived near Tempe, about eight minutes away by car.

Though Tempe felt sure the firemen's efforts were futile, they continued their resuscitation attempt.

"This certainly isn't doing my business any good," Claudia said, continuing to pace around the group gathered at her husband's side.

"It might be a good idea if you closed the Inn for the night," Pete suggested.

Claudia raised her eyebrows. "I don't think Andre would like that."

"Mr. Donato won't care," Pete said.

"What do you mean, Captain Roundtree? Why wouldn't he care? What exactly is wrong with my husband?"

Pete was saved from answering by another arrival. A short, portly man with a reddish face and bald head and bushy mustache shoved his way through the swinging doors. "What the hell's going on around here? Has something happened to my wife?" It was Elise's husband, Wilbur Carmony.

"Elise is fine, Wilbur," Tempe said. "See, she's right over there. Andre Donato has the problem."

Wilbur took in the scene. He stared at the fallen man with obvious distaste, and side-stepped around him to where his wife stood weeping. "What's wrong with you?"

Elise shook her head and shrugged away from her husband. Wilbur jammed his hands in his pockets and stared glumly at the firemen who continued to work over Donato's seemingly lifeless body.

Lupe sidled up to Tempe. "Is Mr. Donato going to be all right?"

Tempe slipped her arm around the girl. "I don't know, Lupe. We'll know more when Dr. McClatchey gets here." Tempe could feel the girl trembling, and she seemed unusually pale.

"Are you okay?" Tempe asked, peering at Lupe.

She nodded.

Dr. McClatchey marched in carrying an old-fashioned black medical bag. "Where's the patient?" He didn't need nor wait for an answer, kneeling beside Donato.

The doctor, a big chested man, with thick white hair and a clean shaven face, pulled a stethoscope from his bag. He used it to listen intently in several places on the victim's chest and neck. When he removed the stethoscope from his ears, he stood. "I'm sorry, Mrs. Donato. There's nothing I can do for your husband."

Claudia frowned. "What do you mean? You've got to do something."

"No, my dear, your husband's dead."

"How can that be? He's never been seriously ill in his entire life."

"These things happen." Dr. McClatchey patted her arm. "My guess is the poor man had a stroke."

The new widow frowned at the doctor's announcement. "I don't believe it."

Hutch stepped closer. "Perhaps you should sit down. This has been quite a shock."

"No, I don't want to sit. This is crazy. How can he be gone?"

Hutch tried again. "Please, why don't you..."

"No. No. No." Claudia shook her head.

"If you don't need me any longer..." Dr. McClatchey began.

"Would you mind taking a look at Lupe, doctor? She doesn't seem to be feeling well either," Tempe said.

"Oh, I'm fine, really. I've just got a bit of a headache." Lupe backed away.

"Understandable, considering what just happened here. Take some aspirin and get to bed as soon as you can, my dear," the doctor said, giving the girl a quick glance. He snapped his bag shut.

Turning to Claudia, he said, "Mrs. Donato, I can give you something for your nerves, if you like."

Claudia continued to look puzzled. "No, no. I need to think. Are you sure Andre is dead?"

"Positive, my dear. I'll be leaving if you don't have any further need for me."

Her eyes filled with tears, and she wobbled a bit. Hutch reached out to steady her. "Your husband is in God's hands now." Claudia leaned against him momentarily.

A siren wailed in the distance—the ambulance.

Pulling herself away from Hutch, Claudia said, "Now they come. When it's too late to do anything for Andre."

"I'll fill in the ambulance attendants. " Dr. McClatchey disappeared through the swinging doors.

"I just can't believe Andre is dead," Claudia said to no one in particular.

"Good riddance to bad rubbish, if you ask me," Wilbur muttered.

The unkind words put an abrupt stop to Elise's crying. "Wilbur. What a horrid thing to say!"

"Well, it's true! No one liked the man except you. Everyone knew you had a silly, school girl crush on him."

Hutch moved closer to the couple. "Mr. Carmony, this is neither the time or place for this. Please, have some respect for the widow."

Glowering beneath shaggy eyebrows, Wilbur muttered, "If the truth be known, Mrs. Donato is probably counting her blessings."

The firemen, who were packing up their equipment, looked embarrassed by Carmony's comments.

Elise, her mascara smudged by her tears, glared at her husband.

Hutch frowned at Mr. Carmony.

Claudia Donato continued to stare at Andre's still body in disbelief. Lupe looked green. The rest of the kitchen staff huddled together, whispering.

"Come on, Wilbur. Let's go." Tempe reached toward him.

"All right, you don't have to be so pushy. I'm leaving. Guess it doesn't matter anyway. My wife hasn't got any reason not to come straight home from work anymore." He shoved his way through the swinging doors, plowing into the white-suited ambulance attendants on their way through.

"Excuse us," said one of the attendants, a young, blonde woman.

"Here's the victim," Pete Roundtree pointed out unnecessarily.

Tempe touched Claudia tentatively on the arm. "Why don't we get out of the way. We'll tell your patrons what's happened, and I can help you close."

"I suppose that would be best." Claudia started toward the doorway with Tempe, but turned back to Elise. "See that the kitchen is cleaned, then you can dismiss everyone for the night. I'll let you know sometime tomorrow what I'm going to do."

Elise started to protest, but Tempe and Claudia left before she could say anything.

The few guests remaining were standing in a group talking, they grew silent as Tempe and Claudia entered the dining room. Before Tempe could say anything, Claudia said, "I'm sorry to have to inform you that my husband has passed away unexpectedly. The Inn is closed. When we reopen, you are all invited to have a meal on the house."

Claudia turned to Tempe and lowered her voice. "I'm going to call Nick Two John to help me." She strode away, her high heels clicking on the wood floors.

Surprised by Claudia's quick recovery, Tempe ushered the last of the customers out the front door and put up the CLOSED sign. Pete Roundtree and his volunteer firemen left, followed closely by the ambulance attendants bringing out Andre Donato's blanket-covered corpse.

Stepping into the empty dining room, Hutch smiled sadly, "Our evening certainly didn't turn out the way I'd hoped."

Tempe went to him and he took her into his arms. "Just hold me for a minute."

"Can we leave now?" Hutch asked.

"I don't see why not, no crime has been committed. Claudia seems to be handling the situation quite well. Give me a moment to check on the other women first." She slipped from his embrace.

Poking her head into the kitchen, she saw Elise had recovered sufficiently to snap orders to the kitchen help. Lupe was at the sink with her back to Tempe. Nick Two John rushed in from the parking lot and spotted Tempe.

"Is it true? He's really dead?" Nick sounded incredulous rather than upset by his boss's unexpected demise.

"Yes, he's dead all right," Tempe assured him.

"What happened? Claudia sounded like she didn't quite believe it."

"We don't really know. The doctor said a stroke, maybe."

"Where is she?"

Tempe knew he meant Claudia. He never even glanced in the direction of Elise or Lupe. "She called you from her office."

"If I can be any help, let me know," Hutch said.

"Thanks." Nick strode off.

"Are you going to be all right, Elise?" Tempe asked.

Elise glanced over her shoulder. She sounded angry as she said, "There's nothing you can do for me, Deputy Crabtree."

Elise's change of mood surprised Tempe too. She felt as though there was something more she ought to do, but couldn't think what. Tempe rejoined Hutch. She slipped her arm through his. "I guess we can leave."

He pulled his truck behind her Blazer parked in the driveway of her cottage, and hurried around to open her door.

"Why don't you come in for awhile? I'll make some coffee," Tempe suggested.

Hutch grasped her around the waist and helped her down from the cab. "Sounds good to me."

After she'd poured their coffee, she carried the mugs into the living room where Hutch waited among the multi-colored and patterned pillows piled in the corner of the old plump couch. The flickering light of the fire in the stone fireplace at the far end of the room caused golden highlights to gleam in Hutch's dark auburn hair. He looked comfortably cozy. After setting the mugs on the coffee table in front of the couch, she kicked off her shoes and settled herself next to him.

He slipped his arm around her. "This is more like it. I made a fire. I thought you'd like it."

She put her head against his chest, luxuriating in the warmth and comfort of the moment. "And you were right."

"So when do you think would be a good time to set the date for our wedding?" Hutch asked.

Tempe giggled. "You certainly are persistent, and I love you for it. Let's wait until Blair gets out of school. The end of June or the beginning of July ought to be fine...if I can get the time off then."

"When will you know?"

"Next time I go into the station I'll speak to Sergeant Guthrie, see how the vacation schedule is. If I tell him I'm getting married, that should help."

"That sounds so good." He tipped her chin upwards with his fingers, and pressed his lips against hers. Tempe put her arms around his neck.

Their coffee was soon forgotten as their kiss deepened, hands caressing.

Hutch brushed her cheek with the back of his fingers. "Tempe, I love you so much." His lips parted, and he leaned towards her again.

The phone rang.

"Oh, no, not now," Tempe groaned.

"Why don't you ignore it."

"I'm sorry, I can't. I'm on call you know. It's part of my job." Tempe pulled away from him. The nearest phone was in her bedroom, she hurried to answer it. "Deputy Crabtree here."

"Tempe, this is Nick Two John. I think you better get over here quick."

"What's wrong?"

"Something's happened to Lupe Madrid."

"I'll be right there."

Chapter 5

TEMPE AND Hutch drove to the Inn in the Blazer. The light engine from the fire station that was used for medical emergencies, was parked near the beginning of the Indian trail. Its red light swirled in the darkness. Tempe parked next to it. Claudia stood outlined in the open kitchen door. Obviously she'd been in bed, her blonde hair was mussed, she wore a sashed, black satin negligee, her feet bare.

"They're down the trail on the way to the cabins," Claudia called out to them.

After pulling her flashlight from its holder in her vehicle, Tempe raced down the trail. Hutch followed. The herb and flower garden on each side of the path seemed strangely eerie as her flashlight beam played over the plants, with the shadowed trees looming menacingly in the background.

As they came to the meadow, the trail split. One part continued along the path they'd taken earlier in the day, the other led to the old cabins where Two John and Lupe lived.

Tempe followed the lower trail. As she jogged around the bend, she spotted bobbing lights and dark shapes moving just ahead.

"Deputy Crabtree, is that you?" Nick Two John called out.

"Yes, it's me."

Nick stepped out of the darkness and met her. Worry etched his handsome face. His chest and feet were bare. Despite the cool temperature of the night air, sweat glistened on his bronze skin.

"Lupe is really sick. I found her out here on the trail. Take a look for yourself."

The same volunteers who had come to help Andre Donato earlier, knelt beside Lupe. They had rolled her over on her side. When Tempe got close enough, she leaned over and studied the girl.

Red blotches covered her face and neck, her eyes were closed. Tempe could see Lupe's chest rising and falling. At least she was still alive, thank God. "How's she doing?"

"Lousy," Charlene Goodson said.

"What's the matter with her?" Hutch placed a hand on Tempe's shoulder.

"Looks like she's suffering from the same thing as Mr. Donate. Must be catching." Henley, the other volunteer prepared to take Lupe's blood pressure again.

"She needs to go to the hospital," Charlene added.

Tempe had an idea. "It takes so long for the ambulance to get here, why don't I take her in the Blazer to meet it?"

"Perfect," Charlene said. "I'll radio in and let them know what we're doing. We'll set up a rendezvous point."

While the volunteers lifted Lupe onto the gurney, Tempe turned to Hutch. "Go back to the Inn and give Dr. McClatchey a call. Ask him to meet us at the hospital."

"Right away." Hutch ran back down the trail.

Charlene and Henley rolled the gurney with the unconscious girl toward the parking lot. Tempe turned to Two John. "How did you happen to find her?"

"I was going to my cabin and nearly stumbled over her. She was just lying there. I knew she was really sick because I couldn't rouse her. What do you think is wrong with her? Is she going to die like Donato?"

"I certainly hope not. Thanks for calling me, Nick."

"I thought you ought to know." Two John remained standing in the path as Tempe trotted off.

Lupe had already been loaded in the back seat of the Blazer. Hutch was with Lupe, her head cradled in his arms. "I'll keep an eye on her."

"Good idea. Did you reach the doctor?" Tempe climbed into the front and slammed the door.

"He wasn't happy, but he agreed to meet us at the hospital."

As she backed out of the parking lot, Tempe asked, "What do you suppose is the problem? Something we're going to have to worry about?"

"Too late to worry. If it's contagious we've already been exposed," Hutch said. "Remember Andre complained of a headache...and so did Lupe."

"And she's got the same kind of blotches he did." Tempe switched on her emergency lights and sped down the highway. Behind her, Hutch murmured soothingly to the still unconscious Lupe. "Don't worry, we'll soon have you in good hands. Everything will be all right."

They met the ambulance coming from Dennison near the lake. After hurriedly pulling into the turn-out of the vista point, Hutch helped the attendants transfer Lupe into the back of their vehicle.

"We'll follow you," Tempe hollered as they dashed back to the Blazer.

"I hope you don't mind, but I want to hear what the doctor has to say about Lupe's condition." Tempe pulled in behind the speeding ambulance.

"I want to know too."

During the remainder of the ride to the hospital, neither of them spoke. Hutch seemed to be looking out the passenger window, but Tempe suspected he was praying.

Dr. McClatchey arrived at the hospital moments after they did, an expensive trench coat flapping around his legs, his battered medicine bag in his hand. They met at the automatic doors leading to the main entrance of the emergency room.

"How'd she do on the trip down?" the physician asked as Tempe and Hutch stepped aside to allow him to enter first.

"Remained unconscious," Tempe said, following him. "But at least she's still alive."

Only a few people slouched in the plastic waiting room chairs. A child slept stretched out across the seats of three. Near the ceiling, a television played a late night talk show.

Dr. McClatchey paused at the glassed-in reception desk presided over by a heavy-set nurse with a short kinky perm.

She smiled briefly at him and unlocked the door leading to the inner-sanctum of the emergency room.

She glanced at Tempe and Hutch. "You'll have to wait out..." Frowning, she added, "Oh, Deputy Crabtree, I almost didn't recognize you all dressed up like that."

Tempe knew she looked quite different out of uniform and with her long hair free from its usual braid and brushed out around her shoulders. "I'm here about Doctor McClatchey's patient, as is Pastor Hutchinson."

"You can go in, but you'll both have to stay out of the doctor's way," she said.

She led the trio past several cubicles with their curtains pulled aside, revealing patients of various ages, ailments and injuries.

Pointing to where the ambulance attendants were exiting with the empty gurney, the nurse said, "Your patient is in there, Doctor."

McClatchey stepped into the small area which was occupied by the emergency room doctor. Tempe moved as close as possible without actually stepping inside. She could see Lupe lying still on the examination table, an IV attached to her arm.

The physician on duty reached up and swept the curtain closed giving Tempe a brief view of his youthful, pale face, round glasses perched above a long nose, thin, turned-down lips, and a name tag that read Dr. Taylor. Though they could no longer see what was going on, but they could hear fine.

"Any idea what the problem is, Doc?" Dr. Taylor asked. "Was told you recently had a patient with similar symptoms."

"I can't seem to associate them with any particular malady. When I was called out earlier to Andre Donato's death, I assumed he'd had some sort of stroke. But since this young woman seems to be suffering from the same problem, I've changed my opinion." Rustling sounds accompanied Dr. McClatchey's voice.

"What kind of symptoms are we talking about, Doc?"

"Both complained of headaches. The other patient vomited, don't know about this one."

"Where were they?"

"In the kitchen of a restaurant."

A drawer was opened and shut. "Maybe what we're dealing with here is food poisoning," Dr. Taylor said.

"That's certainly possible. But these splotches make me think she might be allergic to something. We'll pump her stomach to be on the safe side," Dr. McClatchey said.

Frowning, Tempe blurted out, "If it is food poisoning wouldn't you think that some of the other patrons of the Inn would be turning up here with the same symptoms? It seems kind of strange that just two people who worked at the Inn would get sick from the food."

Though the physicians had to have heard, they made no comment.

Tempe continued to mull over the problem. "I feel fine, don't you, Hutch?"

He nodded.

"And we ate a whole meal. Maybe it was something else."

Dr. McClatchey said loudly, "We'll assume it was food poisoning or an allergic reaction until we come up with some other answer."

Moving closer to the curtain separating them from what was going on in the cubicle, Tempe said, "What if it was some sort of poisoning...but not from the food?"

Hutch's auburn brows nearly touched. "You mean someone poisoned Andre and Lupe deliberately?"

"Maybe."

No comment came from the other side.

"Please have the stomach contents analyzed, Doctor," Tempe said.

Dr. McClatchey yanked back the curtain enough to poke his head out. "Of course. We need to know what Miss Madrid ingested. But I think your idea of a deliberate poisoning is rather far-fetched. What reason would anyone have to want either Andre or this young woman dead?"

"I don't know about Lupe, but there's quite a few folks in Bear Creek who weren't all that fond of Andre," Tempe said.

"But was there anyone who disliked him enough to want him dead?" Hutch asked.

"Of course I don't know. But if we discover that Lupe was poisoned then there's a definite possibility Andre was, too."

Dr. McClatchey stared at Tempe skeptically. She knew both of the physicians thought her theory wrong. Though she realized she didn't have any evidence to back it up, she wanted to make sure that if there was any, it would be preserved.

Hutch shifted his position and ran his fingers through his hair. Probably in an effort to change the subject, he asked, "How is Lupe doing now?"

Tempe peered around the doctor and caught a glimpse of Lupe's face. Her coloring had improved, the blotches faded.

Dr. McClatchey didn't move out of the way, but he said, "Her vital signs are strong. I think she'll be fine."

"Thank God," Hutch said, adding, "And both of you doctors also, of course."

"Glad you gave us a little credit, Pastor," Dr. McClatchey said good-naturedly.

"When can I talk to Lupe?" Tempe asked.

"Not tonight," Dr. McClatchey snapped, stepping outside the cubicle, pulling the curtain closed behind him. "She needs lots of rest. Once her condition is stabilized, she'll be transferred to ICU. If she's better in the morning, you can talk to her then."

Tempe thought for a moment. Speaking quietly, she said, "There's not much point in my staying here unless you think her condition might worsen."

Dr. McClatchey raised a white, shaggy eyebrow. "Even in the best of cases there's always the chance a patient might take a turn for the worse, I can't give you any guarantees. However, it is my professional opinion that Miss Madrid will survive whatever this particular malady might be."

"And that's all I can ask for," Tempe said. "Thank you, Doctor." Turning to Hutch, she said, "Let's go. I need some sleep. I want to come back early to see if I can find out anything from Lupe."

On the way home, Hutch asked, "You don't really think someone deliberately poisoned Andre and Lupe, do you?"

"I don't know but it is a possibility. After I hear what the lab discovers from the contents of Lupe's stomach, and I talk to her, I'll know something more definite."

"But Tempe, you're talking about murder and attempted murder."

Tempe kept her eye on the road. "I know."

"Who on earth would want to kill both Andre Donato and Lupe Madrid?"

"It isn't who on earth, but who in Bear Creek. And I don't have any idea. But Hutch, I can't help but remember what Nick Two John said to me after I arrested him."

"What was that?"

"He said there are things going on in Bear Creek that I didn't know about. Things that would affect a lot of people."

"Like what?"

"He would only tell me if I agreed not to book him and of course, I couldn't do that."

"Maybe there really wasn't anything to tell. He might have only said that to influence you to change your mind."

"That's a possibility, of course. But when I didn't, Nick added, 'You're going to be real, real sorry you didn't listen'." Tempe could remember the venom in Two John's voice as he spoke.

She continued, "And what did you think about Claudia in that negligee, and Nick without his shirt, just going back to his place when he found Lupe?"

"I don't even want to speculate."

"I will. It looks like something has been going on between Claudia and Nick Two John."

"You don't suppose he had anything to do with Andre's death..." Hutch let his voice trail off.

"I certainly hope not, but that's something I'll have to find out."

Chapter 6

TEMPE LEFT for the hospital right after Blair climbed on the school bus. Even though it was her second day off, she decided to wear her uniform. Without stopping at the main desk, Tempe hurried down the hallway of Dennison Community Hospital to the Intensive Care Unit. Once there, she had to check in at the nurses' station to get directions to Lupe's room.

A pretty young nurse stood at the open door of a filing cabinet. She either didn't notice—or chose not to notice—Tempe's approach to the counter that set the area apart.

"Excuse me," Tempe began, "I'd like to know where I can find a patient named Lupe Madrid."

Without even turning to look at Tempe, the nurse said, "I'm sorry but that patient is no longer with us."

Tempe's heart sank. Dr. McClatchey had seemed so positive that Lupe was going to make it. "Oh, no!" she gasped. "When did she die?"

The nurse whirled around. "My goodness, she didn't die."

Feeling relieved but confused, Tempe asked, "Well then, what did happen to her?"

"I meant the patient has been moved from ICU onto the ward. I'm so sorry, I didn't mean to upset you."

Tempe nodded, not trusting herself to say anymore than, "Where can I find her?"

The nurse gave her the room number along with directions, and continued to apologize as Tempe strode down the corridor.

She found the room easily and stuck her head in the door. Lupe sat up in bed, her breakfast on the tray in front of her. She grinned when she spotted Tempe peeking around the door.

"Hi, Deputy Crabtree, come on in." Lupe's long black hair curled around her shoulders, and her cheeks had a healthy pink glow. Her dark eyes sparkled. She was obviously happy to see Tempe.

"You certainly look much better than you did last night. How are you feeling?"

"Except for a sore throat, I feel super. I'd offer you some

breakfast but I don't think you'd want what they've given me. I'm starving, and all they bring me is a bowl of lumpy oatmeal and a limp piece of toast." Despite Lupe's complaint she'd already eaten nearly all the cereal, and she popped another spoonful into her mouth.

"I'm glad to hear you're feeling so good."

Nodding, Lupe swallowed. "I hope they'll let me go home. I know Mrs. Carmony must need me, what with Mr. Donato...and all."

"You don't have to be in any hurry to leave, Lupe. We want to make sure that you're all right."

"Truly, I feel terrific. I must've just eaten something that didn't agree with me. The nurse told me they pumped my stomach, so whatever caused the problem is gone."

"That's what I wanted to talk to you about. Since you seemed to have the same symptoms as Mr. Donato, is there something that both of you might have eaten that could have made you sick and killed him?"

Lupe shrugged. "I don't know. I didn't have much of anything last night. And Mr. and Mrs. Donato either eat with special guests in the dining room or alone in their office. Mrs. Carmony fixes their plates and serves them herself. I wait to have my dinner after the last of our guests have been served. But last night, I don't think the Donatos had eaten before he took sick."

"Surely there must have been something that you nibbled on, something that Mr. Donato might have tasted too," Tempe said, disappointed. She'd been positive that once she spoke to Lupe she'd know exactly what it was that had poisoned the girl and her employer.

Frowning, Lupe thought for a moment. "Mrs. Carmony wouldn't like it if she caught the kitchen help sampling the food while we're supposed to be working. Not that we don't sneak a tidbit now and then. But I really don't remember Mr. Donato eating anything that I might have..." She paused and blinked her eyes. "Oh dear."

"What is it?" Tempe moved closer. "What did you remember?"

"I think I know what it was." Lupe looked miserable.

"Tell me, Lupe."

"If Mrs. Carmony finds out I'm going to be in big trouble. She might even fire me."

Feeling impatient, Tempe said, "I doubt that. I'm sure she'll be quite happy if you can help us identify what killed Mr. Donato."

Lupe pushed away the tray with her unfinished breakfast, and swung her legs over the side of the bed. "Promise not to tell Mrs. Carmony, okay?"

"If it was tainted food, Lupe, she'll have to be told."

"It wasn't food."

"Then what was it?"

"Mr. Donato's special iced tea. I didn't mean to drink it. But I'd already poured a glassful when I realized I'd accidentally gotten the pitcher that Mrs. Carmony uses for Mr. Donato's tea. It was easier to drink it than pour it back. That's the only thing I can think of that we both had last night that was the same."

Excited by the information, Tempe asked, "What did it taste like? Was it bitter? Unusually sweet?"

Lupe shrugged. "I don't know. I drank it so fast, I didn't really take the time to taste it."

"Did everyone know that particular pitcher was reserved for Mr. Donato's tea?" Tempe asked.

"Oh, sure. The different kinds of iced teas we make up ahead of time are kept in plastic jugs with lids on them and they are labeled. Mr. Donato's tea was kept in a cut- glass pitcher with a sterling silver rim. There really wasn't any way to mistake it except I wasn't paying attention when I grabbed it out of the refrigerator. I was thirsty, and I didn't think it would make any difference if I drank only one little glass."

Tempe didn't think it necessary to remind Lupe that her mistake sent her to the hospital. "Did Mr. Donato make his own tea?"

"He was real particular about how it was made but Mrs. Carmony was the one who always did it." Lupe pushed her curly hair back from her face. "I probably shouldn't say this, but Mrs. Carmony kind of had a crush on Mr. Donato. She was always super nice to him."

"Yes, I've heard that before. What about him? Did he like her too?"

"Not the same way." Lupe sighed. "Oh, I think he did sleep with her. He took advantage of the way she felt about him. But he flirted a lot with everyone...even me. I'm sure if I'd shown the least bit of interest, he would have tried to get me in bed too." She made a face.

"Andre did have a reputation for being a womanizer."

"I really want to go home, Deputy Crabtree. Do you suppose you could find out when I can?"

"Sure, I'll go ask a nurse. I'm going back up to Bear Creek, if we can get you checked out of here, I'll take you with me."

"That would be so great."

Tempe found an orderly who paged Dr. McClatchey. He was making morning rounds before going back home to his office. The white haired physician bustled into Lupe's room. "What is this I hear about you wanting to leave?"

"I feel perfect, truly I do," Lupe said. "Can I go home?"

"You certainly seem to have recovered." He glanced over her chart, murmuring, "Um hum...um hum...um hum."

"If you'll okay it, I can take her home," Tempe said, in an effort to hurry him along. She was anxious to get back to the Inn and recover the pitcher of iced tea. The contents should be analyzed.

"I can't see any reason why we should keep you here any longer. You go ahead and get dressed and I'll sign your discharge papers."

"Oh, thank you," Lupe squealed as she slid from the bed.

Tempe followed the physician from the room. "Excuse me, doctor, have you heard anything from the lab yet? About the contents of Lupe's stomach?"

"It's much too soon, Deputy Crabtree. I promise I'll let you know as soon as I receive a report."

While Tempe drove them back to Bear Creek, Lupe alternately picked at her nails and twisted a black curl in her fingers. Finally she said, "Deputy Crabtree, is it possible...could you please not... well, I really don't know how to say it..."

"What is it?" Tempe glanced at the girl. She looked like she was in pain. "Lupe? You're not getting sick again, are you? I can turn around right now and take you back to..."

"No, no, I'm fine, really I am. But I don't want you to tell Mrs. Carmony about me drinking Mr. Donato's tea. She warned us over and over not to touch it. If she finds out what I did...even though it was an accident...I'm not kidding, she'll fire me. I can't afford to lose my job."

Tempe sympathized with her but didn't think there was any way to keep the information away from Elise Carmony. "I won't make an issue of it, Lupe, but eventually she'll find out. Especially if it turns out that the tea was poisoned."

Lupe slumped in her seat and stared out the window.

"Look Lupe, don't worry, if it comes to that...and I don't think it will...I'll help you find another job and a place to live."

Tempe didn't know if Andre Donato had been deliberately poisoned, and even if she did it wasn't her job to investigate, but she wanted to ask Lupe the questions that had been plaguing her. If it turned out that Donato had been murdered, any information she was able to gather the sheriff department's homicide detectives would be glad to hear.

"So tell me, Lupe, if Mr. Donato's tea was poisoned, who do think might have done it?"

Lupe turned toward Tempe, her eyes huge. "Is that what you think? Someone murdered Mr. Donato?"

"We won't know until we get the results of the lab tests. Even then it might not be conclusive. But it is a possibility. Do you know of anyone who disliked your boss enough to kill him?"

Lupe bowed her head, her thick curls hiding her expression from Tempe. "Uh-uh."

Tempe suspected that Lupe was lying in an effort to protect someone. "Well, tell me this then. Who could have come into the kitchen and put something into the tea without being noticed?"

Shrugging, the girl said, "Anyone. The Donatos lock the front door of the Inn when it isn't open, but they never lock the kitchen door. You know how it is here in Bear Creek. Hardly anyone locks up."

"Yes, I know." Tempe wasn't thrilled with the practice. The old-timers remembered the days when Bear Creek had little crime, and the refugees from the big cities had a false sense of security thinking they'd left all the criminals behind. Unfortunately, the mountain community was close enough for any burglar or thief to easily make the commute—which they did often enough to keep Tempe busy.

Tempe realized that anyone could have entered the kitchen of the Inn during the night or early in the morning and added something to Andre Donato's pitcher of tea. It would have to have been someone who knew about it—but anyone who came to the Inn to eat probably did. After all, he'd made a point to mention it to Tempe and Hutch the night before. And it wouldn't take a great deal of brains to figure out that the cut glass pitcher held the special brew.

So far her sleuthing hadn't profited her with any real answers to the dilemma.

After pulling into the lot behind the Inn, Tempe parked the Blazer next to the Donatos' cars near the back door. "Here you are, Lupe. Are you going to be able to walk all the way to your cabin by yourself, or do you want me to go with you?"

"Oh, I can make it. Honestly, I feel great. A little weak maybe...but I think that's because they tried to starve me in the hospital." Lupe opened the door and jumped down.

"I think I'll go inside and see how Mrs. Donato is doing," Tempe said.

Hesitating before taking off, Lupe said, "Tell her I'm okay, and if she needs me to do anything, anything at all, to give me a call."

Tempe nodded, and Lupe hurried off toward the trail which led through the herb and flower garden.

Tempe found the back door unlocked and no one in the kitchen. She walked over to the large double-doored stainless steel refrigerator and opened the left side. The top shelf held several plastic jugs labeled rose hip, sweet clover, camomile. But she didn't see the fancy pitcher Lupe had described. Tempe poked around the various bowls and containers until she was certain it wasn't on any of the shelves on either side of the refrigerator.

She turned around, put her hands on her hips and surveyed the kitchen. In an enormous dish drainer on the sink, turned upside down and nestled in among coffee cups and assorted dishes, was the cut glass pitcher with a silver rim. Tempe knew it was the one that had held the special iced tea. So much for testing the contents. She wondered who dumped and washed it. And did it matter?

Disappointed, Tempe shoved her way through the swinging doors and stepped into the cavernous dining room. The tables were still covered with the linen cloths, and the vases still held the single Lily of the Valley, though the bell-shaped blossoms had wilted and drooped low on their stems.

Tempe wondered if she would find Claudia Donato in her office or upstairs in the suite of rooms where she and her husband had made their home. As she approached the office, she heard voices. When she knocked, the door, which hadn't been closed tightly, swung open.

Nick Two John held Claudia in his arms. Both of them turned their startled faces toward her, and Nick quickly released Claudia and stepped away. He grinned sheepishly as he tucked his chambray shirt into his Levis. Looking more like a haughty aristocrat than a newly-bereaved widow, Claudia raised her pointed chin and narrowed her long-lashed eyes while quickly smoothing her sleek, silk blouse.

"What right do you have to barge in here like this, Deputy Crabtree?" she snapped.

"Excuse me, I merely knocked and the door came open by itself. I want to ask you a few questions," Tempe said.

"Why on earth would I want to talk to you?" she snapped. "Get out. Can't you see I'm busy?" Claudia fluffed her shoulder-length blonde tresses with her fingers before stepping behind her desk.

Without glancing at Tempe, Two John smiled at Claudia, revealing his straight, white teeth. "Why don't you humor the deputy, Mrs. Donato? What can it hurt. I'll be around if you need me."

"Wait, Nick. I really don't want..." Claudia began but Nick swaggered toward the door, his thick, long braids swinging against his broad back. Before he closed the door, she added hurriedly, "Check back with me later, I'll probably have something for you to do."

Claudia crossed her arms and stared at Tempe. "I have a hell of a lot of work to do here even though I just lost my husband. Fortunately, Nick is lending a hand in that department."

And in another department too, obviously. "It's your husband's death that I want to talk to you about, Mrs. Donato."

Sighing, Mrs. Donato dropped into her chair. "For goodness sake, why don't you stop the Mrs. Donato bit and just call me Claudia, and I'll call you Tempe. All right?"

"Fine, Claudia it is."

"What is it you want to know about my husband's death, Tempe? You were right there when it happened, just like I was. Surely you know as much as I do about it."

There was no need to worry about the woman's feelings, obviously she wasn't suffering over the loss of her spouse. "I have reason to believe that your husband may have been murdered. Did he have any enemies?"

Tempe was surprised by Claudia's reaction. She turned pale beneath her make-up, her eyes opened wide, and her mouth dropped open. "Oh, my God! No! Surely he wouldn't have. There was no need! Oh, my God!"

Chapter 7

"WHO IS IT that you think might be responsible for your husband's death, Claudia?" Tempe asked, moving directly across the desk in order to watch her reactions more closely.

A hand flew to Claudia's mouth as if sorry she'd spoken, but when she removed it she'd regained her composure though not her coloring. "You might as well know...my husband had many enemies."

"Tell me about them." Tempe pulled a small notebook and pen from her breast pocket. "Do you mind if I sit down?"

Claudia shook her head and began rummaging in the top drawer of the desk until she found what she was looking for. "Here, read this." She thrust a piece of tan paper at Tempe.

With words drawn to look like logs, the letterhead read VAN TASSEL MILL, followed by a Bear Creek address. Beneath, scrawled in large handwriting were the words, "Don't even think about selling to Bazmanian. You're life won't be worth a plug nickel. Van".

"May I take this letter?" Tempe asked.

"Sure. I have no use for it. The only reason Andre kept it was because he thought it was funny. I think he planned to use it against Mr. Van Tassel in some manner."

"Was your husband really planning to sell the Inn to Mr. Bazmanian?" He was a wealthy financier and developer headquartered in Visalia.

"My husband was always looking for a way to make a profit. Bazmanian came here to see him. He offered Andre an enormous amount of money for the Inn and the land surrounding it."

"Was Andre planning on accepting the offer?"

"He certainly contemplated the idea. But he hadn't come to any decision as far as I know."

"How did you feel, Claudia?" Tempe asked.

"I didn't really have an opinion on the matter," Claudia said, turning her head away from Tempe. "I never really wanted to move from southern California in the first place. Bear Creek is much too back-woodsy for my tastes. There's absolutely no culture and the people are unsophisticated. I've had to create my own pleasures and diversions."

Tempe immediately thought of Nick Two John. Claudia colored slightly, and quickly stood, to fiddle with an oil painting hanging on the wall behind her.

When she turned back around, she said, "On the other hand, I've worked really hard to turn the Inn into a place where all you unfortunates that live around here can be exposed to some elegance and class if only for a short while. I wasn't really ready to give that up. But to be perfectly frank, Tempe, Andre hadn't asked my opinion in the matter."

Tempe chose not to comment on Claudia's demeaning assessment of Bear Creek. When she was married to Milt they'd made their home in southern California. She didn't miss anything about it. The natural beauty of the surrounding mountains more than made up for anything Bear Creek lacked.

"How many others knew about Bazmanian's offer?"

Claudia shrugged. "I have no idea. But if Van Tassel knew, I suppose a lot of other people in Bear Creek did too. You know how gossip travels up here."

Yes, Tempe did know, but she wondered why she hadn't heard. "Just when was this offer made to your husband?"

"I don't remember the exact day. Some time last week."

That would explain it, the news just hadn't gotten completely around yet. But she knew Nick Two John would have been one of the first to know because of his relationship to Claudia.

"What kind of plans did Bazmanian have for the Inn?" Tempe asked.

"You have to realize that Andre didn't confide in me at all when it came to business matters," Claudia said. Her expression displayed resentment toward her husband even though he was dead. "I overheard Bazmanian saying something about tearing down this beautiful building. He wanted to construct some ugly modern monstrosity of a hotel. He said something about a golf course and developing the rest of the acreage into expensive condominiums and single family homes."

That information wouldn't have set well with most of the Bear Creek residents. The old-timers especially didn't take kindly to outsiders proposing any sort of business venture that would greatly change the quiet mountain community.

"What did Two John have to say about Bazmanian's plans?" Again, Tempe watched Claudia's face carefully.

The only alteration to her expression was a quick blink and a lift of her chin. "Of course he wasn't happy about it. You know as well as I do how Nick feels about protecting the land. After all, you are the one who arrested him when he was demonstrating against the loggers."

Before Tempe could ask any more questions, her pager beeped. "May I use your phone? The department is trying to reach me."

"Of course."

Tempe dialed the station and found out that Dr. McClatchey had left a message for her to call." She located the physician at his office.

"Yes, indeed, my dear," he said. "I have some intriguing news for you."

Not able to keep the excitement she felt out of her voice, she said, "You've heard from the lab."

"Yes, indeed. I know what caused the Madrid girl's illness." He paused dramatically.

"Tell me."

"It was most definitely poison. A glycoside called convallatoxin, similar to digitalis."

Tempe frowned. "Isn't digitalis a medicine?"

"Yes, but what it has in common with convallatoxin is that they both are derived from plants. Digitalis, of course, comes from foxglove."

"And this convalla...whatever, comes from what?"

"The Lily of the Valley."

Tempe immediately thought of the wilted flowers remaining on each of the tables in the dining room. She was also reminded of Nick Two John describing the various attributes and dangers of all the plants along his Indian trail, including the Lily of the Valley.

"Please, Dr. McClatchey, repeat the name of that poison and spell it for me." She carefully wrote the information down. "There should be an autopsy done on the body." Because the physician had been present at Donato's death, no autopsy had been ordered.

"I've already taken care of it."

"Great. Let me know as soon as you hear anything."

After she hung up, she turned to Claudia. "Thank you for being so cooperative, but I have to go. May I use the phone once more please?"

"Of course, but what's going on? Were you talking about my husband? What did you find out? What's this about an autopsy?"

"I can't tell you anything just yet." Turning her back on Claudia's angry expression, Tempe quickly dialed the number of the sub-station and asked for Sergeant Guthrie.

When he came on the line, he said, "I thought this was your day off, Crabtree. What's going on?"

Claudia moved around where she could watch Tempe.

"I have some important information but I can't explain now. It's something that I think the homicide detectives should hear."

"Does this have something to do with the Donato death?"

"Yes, sir. And there's something else, Dr. McClatchey has ordered an autopsy."

"I'm eager to hear your news, Crabtree."

With hands on her hips, Claudia pushed her face close to Tempe's. "What is all this about an autopsy? This is my husband you're discussing, after all. I have the right to know what's going on."

"Claudia, I'm sorry, but I really can't talk about it just yet. I promise I'll let you know as soon as I can."

"Maybe I'll just call a lawyer and see what my rights are," Claudia snapped.

"That might be a good idea," Tempe said. She paused when she reached the door. "By the way, I brought Lupe back from the hospital. She seems to be fine. She said if you need her for anything to give her a call."

Before Claudia could say anything further, Tempe slipped out of the door.

SERGEANT GUTHRIE leaned back in the chair behind his desk, his hands cradling his head. His bushy, graying eyebrows lifted as he waited for Tempe to begin speaking.

Guthrie and the two detectives were already crowded in the tiny office when Tempe entered. She quickly sat in the one remaining chair.

Richards, wearing a navy blue suit, a light blue striped shirt and a blue tie, was the closest to Tempe. He crossed his long legs, and squinted at her. He always did. Tempe suspected he needed glasses. "So what's this all about, Crabtree?"

"There's good reason to believe Andre Donato was murdered," she said.

Detective Morrison's gray suit didn't conceal his linebacker's build though his ugly face was like a prize fighter's. He growled, "That's the guy who owned the Bear Creek Inn. Thought he died from a stroke or something."

"That's what we all thought last night. But one of the waitresses became ill later on, and had to be taken to the hospital. She had the same symptoms as Mr. Donato. The doctor pumped her stomach and had the contents analyzed. She was poisoned."

The Sergeant sat up straight and brushed the top of his short, military haircut. "And that's why the doctor ordered the autopsy for Donato."

"What kind of poison are we talking about here?" Morrison asked.

Tempe pulled her notebook from her pocket and flipped it open. "It's a glycoside called convallatoxin."

"What the hell's that?" Richards snapped.

Referring to her notes, Tempe repeated all that Dr. McClatchey had told her, ending with, "The poison comes from the Lily-of-the Valley."

"I don't know nothing about flowers." Morrison shifted positions. His coat swung open to reveal his shoulder holster. "You got Lily-of-the Valley in Bear Creek?"

"There's a garden full of them behind the Inn," Tempe said.

"H'mmm," Sergeant Guthrie said. "No wonder the doctor ordered an autopsy. But what's the connection between the waitress and her boss? How did they get a hold of this poison anyhow?"

"Do you want to hear what I think?" Tempe asked, knowing that she really didn't have any evidence to back up her theory.

"Go right ahead," Morrison said, crossing his muscular arms over his broad chest.

"Donato habitually drank a special iced tea that was kept in a cut glass pitcher in the Inn's refrigerator. Lupe, the waitress, drank some of that iced tea. I think that's where the poison was."

"So did you find the pitcher so we can have the tea analyzed?" the Sergeant asked.

Tempe smiled sadly. "I found the pitcher. The tea had been dumped out and the pitcher washed."

"Too bad," Richards said. "Who had access to the kitchen?"

"Just about anyone who wanted to get in there. Lupe told me that they never lock the back door."

"That doesn't help. He have any enemies?" Morrison asked.

"Actually, there may have been quite a few," Tempe said. "Just before I came down here, his wife gave me this." She handed the letter written by Edgar Van Tassel to the Sergeant. He read it and passed it along to the detectives.

"The wife let you in on what Van Tassel was referring to?" Guthrie asked.

"Yes, Andre had been approached by Bazmanian, the big developer, to sell the Inn and the surrounding acreage," Tempe explained.

"Why would Van Tassel care? He might have gotten some business taking down all the trees." Richards looked bored with the whole subject.

"I think his big objection is the same most anyone would have who lives in Bear Creek. No one wants to see that kind of change in the community. Including me."

"Do you think this Van Tassel fellow really meant it when he said Donato's life wouldn't be worth a plug nickel?" Morrison asked.

"Oh, I'm sure he really meant it. But Donato hadn't made up his mind whether or not to sell. I doubt if Van Tassel poisoned him."

Still acting as though he wasn't much interested in Donato's death, Richards asked, "So is there anyone else who might have wanted Donato dead enough to do something about it?"

Though Tempe didn't want to implicate Nick Two John, she knew as soon as the detectives started asking questions in Bear Creek they'd find out everything she knew she had to tell them. "Probably the most likely suspect is Nick Two John."

"He's that Indian you arrested the other day for slashing tires at that Save the Forest Demonstration." Guthrie stated. He pulled a yellow legal pad closer and began taking notes.

"Nick Two John is employed at the Inn. It looks like he and Mrs. Donato have been having an affair. And he's really into the environment. Any plans Andre Donato had for selling the Inn to someone who planned on developing the area would have really upset him."

"Do you think this Two John guy was the one who poisoned Donato's tea?" For the first time Richards sounded like he might be taking an interest in the case.

Tempe shook her head. "If Nick had killed Donato, I think it would have been in a more physical manner. Poisoning doesn't seem like Nick's style. However, I have to tell you that he probably knows more about plants and flowers than anyone in Bear Creek. He's really an expert on the subject. He's the one who planted and cares for the Inn's gardens."

"If it turns out Andre Donato was poisoned, it sounds like Nick Two John is our man," Sergeant Guthrie said.

When she'd told them about Nick, Tempe had known that was the conclusion they would come to. "There's more. Not only did anyone who wanted have access to the Inn's kitchen, but nearly everyone in Bear Creek has taken Nick's Indian trail walk."

"So what's that supposed to mean?" Richards was back to sounding bored.

"What it means is, that anyone who ever went on Nick's walk knows all about the Lily of the Valley being poisonous."

"And who else might have a motive for killing Donato besides Two John and Van Tassel?" Morrison asked.

"I'm not sure."

"Thanks for the information, Crabtree," Guthrie said, standing, letting her know she was being dismissed. "If the autopsy report shows that Donato was poisoned, Detectives Morrison and Richards will proceed with the investigation. If you should come across anything else that might shed some light on the case, call one of them. Keeping those Bear Creek cowboys and rednecks in line is enough to keep you occupied."

Guthrie's manner irritated her, as it often did. He just couldn't get used to having a female deputy. She started to leave without saying anything, but she remembered her promise to Hutch and turned around. "By the way, Sergeant. I'd like a couple of weeks off at the end of June or the beginning of July."

"Oh, yeah? So would most of my deputies. Got something special planned, Crabtree?"

"Yes, as a matter of fact, I do. I'm getting married. Is that special enough?" She couldn't help grinning as she left the three men staring after her, their mouths gaping.

Chapter 8

USING A HOE, Nick chopped at the weeds beginning to sprout at the base of the basil plants. He was shirtless. Sweat glistened on the bronze skin of his back.

Tempe didn't call out to him, and her approach had been quiet, but as soon as she neared him, he stopped and turned toward her. He smiled in a quizzical manner. "I knew you'd be coming around some time today."

"How could you possibly know that?"

"Figured you'd have some questions for me." He leaned on the handle of the hoe.

"You figured right. I have several. And I also want to give you a warning."

Two John remained impassive.

"I've just come from the sub-station, Nick. Your boss was poisoned. The poison came from the Lily of the Valley. The homicide detectives will probably be up here soon to talk to you."

A shadow briefly darkened Two John's eyes.

"You knew what Mr. Donato planned for the Inn, didn't you," she said as a statement rather than a question.

Hate glimmered in Nick's dark eyes as a deep line creased his brow. "Damn right, I knew. The fool was selling out. The buyer was going to cut down all these beautiful trees, tear up my gardens. Ruin everything."

Tempe stared at Nick, wondering if his feelings could have been strong enough to drive him to murder.

Though she hadn't said anything, Nick's expression softened. "I didn't kill him, Tempe. I've never killed anyone in my life."

"I believe you, Nick. But I think the detectives are already considering you as the primary suspect."

Nick nodded. "Figures."

"The best way I know to help you is to find out who the real killer is."

"How do you plan to do that?"

Tempe shrugged. "The same way any crime is solved. Mostly luck and finding the answers to a lot of questions. You've got some of the answers I need."

"Is that right?" Two John appeared amused.

"Yes, Nick. Remember when you told me that you gave me the opportunity to prevent what was about to happen in Bear Creek? Did you know that Andre Donato was going to die?"

Nick put down his hoe. "Why don't we find a cooler spot?"

He led her to a grassy area beneath an oak tree with a rough bench built around it. "Sit down."

Tempe did as she was bid, and Nick crouched in the grass in front of her.

"Of course I didn't know about Donato. But I knew something was about to happen. I could feel the tension in the atmosphere. Like when there's lots of electricity in the air just before a thunderstorm." Nick probed at a weed with his fingers.

"You sounded a lot more certain at the time, Nick. You said there were many things going on in Bear Creek that I didn't know about. What else is going on besides Donato's plan to sell the Inn?"

Standing, Nick brushed the dirt off his hands. "Remember, I was trying to keep you from taking me to jail."

"So you were just making up those threats?" Tempe looked up at Two John but couldn't make eye contact because he stared at the sky, one hand shading his view.

Tempe followed his gaze. Before diving toward its unsuspecting prey, a hawk banked in front of thunder clouds backed up against the mountains.

"Finding out is your job, isn't it?" he asked.

"Actually, it isn't."

Nick turned toward her, his stare penetrating. "I don't understand."

"It's the detectives' job to find out who killed Donato. I'm only supposed to enforce the law, keep the peace, and help out folks in trouble. And I think you might be in trouble, Nick. Why don't you let me help you?"

"I don't need your help, Crabtree."

Tempe clasped her hands. "Okay, if that's what you want. But I still need yours. How would someone extract the poison from the Lily of the Valley?"

"Any number of ways."

"Tell me an easy one."

"The water from a vase the flower has been in contains enough poison to kill someone." Turning abruptly, Nick strode away from Tempe and quickly disappeared from sight.

It irritated her that he'd left her with so many questions. Somehow she should have been able to get through to him that it would have been far better to answer her, to give her something to go on, maybe even some other suspects to investigate. As it was now, all of the evidence pointed toward Two John.

Tempe hurried down the path Nick had taken but didn't catch up with him. Her pager beeped and she decided to use the Inn's phone again. When she entered the kitchen, she was surprised to see Elise Carmony bustling about.

The woman turned, looking startled. "Oh, it's you, Deputy." Her large eyes were red-rimmed and she wasn't wearing any make-up. Elise seemed to be grieving over Mr. Donato's death far more than his widow.

"I need to use the phone," Tempe said.

"Help yourself. You know where it is." Elise pulled a tissue from the pocket of her apron and wiped at a tear.

Tempe dialed the station and was told to call Dr. McClatchey.

The physician had the results of the autopsy. "Just like we thought, Deputy Crabtree. Andre Donato died of convallatoxin poisoning."

"Would you please let Sergeant Guthrie at the sub-station know that Donato was murdered?"

Elise gasped. She'd obviously been eavesdropping. When Tempe hung up, Elise said, "Is it true? Someone killed Andre?"

"I'm afraid so."

"I can't believe it."

"I've been told that you are the one who always made Andre's special tea."

Frowning, Elise nodded. "Yes, that's true. He constantly wanted something non-alcoholic on hand to drink.
I had a special mix of herbal tea that he really liked. I'm the only one who knew how to make it to suit him."

"Probably his tea was poisoned," Tempe said.

Elise gasped. Her hand flew to her ample chest as she took a step backwards. "Oh, you can't possibly think...I wouldn't have done such a thing. I loved Andre...and he loved me."

Looking embarrassed by her confession, and possibly in an attempt to cover that embarrassment, Elise said quickly, "How do you know the tea was poisoned?"

Tempe thought about Lupe's fear of losing her job if Mrs. Carmony knew she'd sampled some of the tea so decided not to mention it. "There's been an autopsy."

"Oh, my God. They cut up my darling's body." Elise's eyes opened even wider, and she looked like she might be sick.

"Is there anyone you know of who might have hated Mr. Donato enough to kill him?" Tempe asked.

Without hesitating, Elise said, "Yes. My husband, Wilbur. He was jealous of Andre. He suspected we were having an affair. And he was angry because he'd heard Andre planned on selling the Inn to some big developer. Wilbur leased grazing land from Andre."

Perhaps Wilbur would have killed Andre because the man was having an affair with his wife—though Tempe thought he would have used a gun instead of poison. But she doubted if the loss of his grazing land was motive enough for murder. There was plenty available around Bear Creek.

Another question came to mind. "Who took care of the flowers for the dining room?"

Appearing momentarily startled, a smile slowly lifted the corners of Elise's lips. "That was Mrs. Donato's job. She was very particular about the flowers. Surely you don't think she..."

"What do you think?"

"I wouldn't want to gossip. But it isn't any secret that she didn't love Andre. I think she just married him for his money. And everyone knows about her and Nick Two John. It was so humiliating for Andre the way his wife acted around that Indian." Elise seemed to have recovered from her sadness.

"Andre actually complained to you about Nick and his wife?" Tempe asked.

"Not in so many words. He didn't have to. I could see how it hurt him when he saw how his wife looked at Two John. And you couldn't help but hear last night when Andre was yelling at her for bailing Two John out of jail."

"Yes, I heard him too," Tempe said.

She glanced at her watch. What she'd like to do was try to find Wilbur Carmony and Edgar Van Tassel and ask them both a few questions. But it was her day off, and she wasn't supposed to be investigating the murder anyway. Now that the results from the autopsy were in, it wouldn't be long before Morrison and Richards made an appearance in Bear Creek. It would be a good idea if she stayed out of their way.

"Do you know if Mrs. Donato plans to open the restaurant any time soon?" Tempe asked.

Elise rolled her eyes. "She plans to reopen tonight. I think it's obscene. She ought to at least wait until after the funeral but she won't listen to me. She reminded me I was just the hired help. I'd like to see her run this place without me."

Though surprised by the news, Tempe made no further comment. If she hurried, she might be able to get some laundry done before Blair came home. She hadn't planned anything for dinner either, and decided to stop by the store first.

As she parked outside the small market tucked between the fire station and the beauty parlor, she spotted Hutch's old blue-and-white Ford truck. He was just climbing into it. Her heart leaped as it always did when she saw him.

She waved and called out, "Hey, Hutch."

"Tempe." His huge grin displayed his pleasure. "I've been trying to call you. What are you doing in uniform? Aren't you supposed to be off today?"

"Yes, I'm supposed to be off." She kissed his cheek. "But I brought Lupe home from the hospital."

"How is she?"

"Doing fine." She glanced around to make sure no one was within hearing, and lowered her voice. "Andre Donato was poisoned."

Hutch put his arm around her. "Oh, dear Lord. Who would have done such a thing?"

She shrugged.

"So what are you planning?"

Smiling, she said, "After I pick up a few groceries, I'm going home to change and enjoy my free evening. I know, why don't you come for dinner tonight? I'll get some steaks."

His gray eyes twinkled. "That sounds terrific. What time?"

After they made the arrangements, they kissed goodbye and Tempe went in the store to do her shopping. When she came out, juggling two full shopping bags she nearly ran into Wilbur Carmony. "Oops, sorry," she said.

The red-faced, bald and mustached man blocked her way. "I hear you been asking questions about me."

Tempe guessed he'd spoken with his wife. She nodded.

"If you've got anything to say to me or about me, Deputy Crabtree, do it right here and now."

"I guess you've heard that Mr. Donato was murdered."

"That's what Elise told me."

"I remember what you said last night when Mr. Donato died."

"Yep, and I meant it. That man planned to sell the Inn to some damn developer. Let me tell you, it would only happen over my dead body."

Tempe adjusted the sacks in her arms. "Elise says you were pretty angry because of the affair she was having with Mr. Donato."

Wilbur snorted. "She told you that? I wasn't mad, just embarrassed for her. The man made a fool of her and she was too dumb to realize it."

Chapter 9

"THE STEAK was great," Blair said. "Sure glad you were here, Hutch. Mom hardly ever barbecues anything but hot dogs."

Despite the clouds butting against the mountains, the May evening was warm and Tempe had decided to eat outside; Hutch offered to do the meat.

"For goodness sake, Blair, you make it sound like I can't cook," Tempe said. "I've never seen you turn down a steak I've broiled in the oven."

Blair hugged her. "I'm not complaining about the way you cook, Mom, honest. But you have to admit, dinner was fantastic."

"Yes, I agree. You did a terrific job, Hutch. And we thank you."

Hutch grinned, dimples deepening.

Tempe loved his smile. She loved him.

"I'll have to show off more of my culinary talents. I'm enjoying all the accolades."

"When are you guys getting married?" Blair asked as he stacked the empty plates. "It's going to be kind of nice to have someone else around who knows how to cook. Maybe I won't have to eat so many microwaved dinners."

"Blair. You make it sound like I don't ever cook. Hutch might change his mind about marrying me." Tempe felt her cheeks flush, and punched her son playfully in the bicep.

"Don't worry. I've been invited to eat here enough to know that you are very talented in that department," Hutch said. "But how about answering your son's question...when are we getting married?"

"I don't have a date yet, but I did tell the Sergeant that I wanted my vacation the end of June or the beginning of July."

"Super." Blair set the dishes down and hugged his mother and Hutch. "It's about time."

"I couldn't agree more," Hutch said. "When will you know the exact date? We must make some arrangements for the wedding. I'll have to find a minister to marry us and substitute for the Sundays I'm gone."

"The next time I go down to the sub-station I'll pin Guthrie down. He seemed rather stunned by my news." Remembering the dumbfounded expressions on the faces of the Sergeant and the detectives when she'd told them why she wanted time off made Tempe chuckle.

"I'll clean up tonight," Blair said. "You two stay out here and do whatever. I have to study for a final."

"Why, Blair, how thoughtful," Tempe said, astounded. Blair's helpfulness leaned more toward yard work and fixing things—and usually only after frequent prodding on her part.

Blair winked and made an okay sign with his thumb and forefinger before scooping up the stack of dishes and heading for the kitchen door. Tempe beamed. It was so wonderful that Blair finally accepted Hutch. He even seemed anxious for them to marry. Her heart swelled with happiness.

"Hutch, do you want more coffee?"

"Nope. I've had plenty for now. Why don't we take a walk down by the river?"

Tempe took his offered arm.

Bear Creek was still swollen from the winter rains, cascading over rocks as it rushed past Tempe's cottage. He guided her down the rough steps carved into the hillside leading down to the steep bank. Cottonwoods, oaks and a few pines lined either side.

The sun had disappeared behind the mountains, leaving the faint glow of twilight. It seemed as though civilization had disappeared as Tempe and Hutch stood on the grassy slope with nothing visible but the sparkling water and the surrounding trees.

Hutch pulled Tempe into his arms. His voice husky, and his mouth near her ear, he said, "I love you. I can hardly wait until we're husband and wife."

"I love you, too, Hutch." Tempe lifted her face to his.

Hutch kissed her lightly several times before settling his lips on hers for a long and lingering kiss.

Too soon, he pulled away from the embrace and took her hand. "Why don't we find some place to sit?" He turned away from her and began looking for a likely spot.

Tempe smiled to herself as he led her to a mossy outcropping below the outstretched limbs of a silver oak.

"This looks good," he said, pulling her down beside him. "Why don't we make some decisions about our wedding? As soon as we know the date I'll make the necessary arrangements. I can hardly wait. You do want to get married in the chapel, don't you."

"Of course. I'd like for it to be a simple ceremony."

"Me too, but you do realize that everyone in Bear Creek will expect an invitation."

"I know you're right but I was hoping for something smaller, a little more intimate."

"Since it's inevitable that we'll be entertaining most of Bear Creek, why don't we ask Claudia Donato if we can have the reception at the Inn?" Hutch suggested. "That's about the only place that's big enough."

Tempe rested against Hutch's shoulder, his arm around her. "I'm not so sure Claudia is going to want to have anything to do with me after today."

"Why is that?"

"I had to tell Sergeant Guthrie and the homicide detectives what I knew about Nick Two John. I'm afraid he looks like the prime suspect in Donato's murder."

"And you don't think he did it?"

"No, I don't. But with so much evidence against him, I'm afraid the detectives aren't going to be looking very hard for anyone else."

"No matter how it works out, I'm sure Claudia will be willing to put on our reception for us. She's already asked me to do her husband's funeral."

"Really? When is that going to be?"

"Day after tomorrow. She just wants something simple at the grave site."

"Andre's going to be buried in the little cemetery behind the chapel? Oh, my goodness, he'll turn over in his coffin once he finds out he's going to end up in Bear Creek permanently."

With an odd tone in his voice, Hutch said, "Tempe, you do realize that Andre isn't going to be around to really care where his body is, don't you?"

"Of course, I was just making a joke." Tempe felt a bit uneasy. She and Hutch really hadn't had an in depth discussion about her beliefs. Though she certainly believed in God, her faith wasn't anywhere near the level of Hutch's. She knew exactly what his convictions were about God, salvation, grace, and life after death because she'd heard him preach often on the subjects.

This was one of those times when she wondered if she ought to speak up about her religious views—or lack of them. Maybe they were too far apart for their marriage to work.

But before she could put her thoughts into words, Hutch said, "Why don't you tell me who you think killed Andre?"

Her curiosity about the same question pushed her concern about her relationship with Hutch into a corner of her mind. "I really don't have a candidate yet, however, my gut feeling is that it wasn't Nick."

"So what all have you found out so far?"

"I'm not supposed to be investigating the murder," Tempe said. "That's the detectives' job. Sergeant Guthrie reminded me quite emphatically."

Hutch squeezed her shoulder. "But I know you, sweetheart. You've been busily asking questions. I saw you with Wilbur Carmony. It didn't look like you were just having a casual conversation."

"I feel like I must find out as much as I can, otherwise, I'm afraid Nick will be arrested and the real murderer will be overlooked."

While they'd been sitting on the riverbank, it became dark. The evening star had been joined by millions of others. It was cooler. Tempe snuggled closer to Hutch.

"So what have you found out so far?"

"When I talked to Elise she implicated her husband. Said he knew she was having an affair with Andre and was mad about that. She also told me that he was even more upset because Andre had been planning to sell the land Wilbur leased for grazing his cattle."

"Seems to me that isn't as much a reason to kill someone as the affair. There's plenty more land around here."

"That's what I thought too. But when I talked to Wilbur he didn't seem upset about Elise and Andre. In fact, he said they weren't really having an affair. That Andre was just playing Elise for a fool."

"I wonder which it was."

"Lupe said Elise had gone to bed with Andre."

"Going to bed with someone and having an affair isn't quite the same thing," Hutch said.

"No, I guess it isn't. Though you'd think either one would be enough to make Wilbur mad at Andre." Tempe shivered.

"You're cold. We'd better go inside."

As they hiked back up the hill toward the house, Tempe said, "And then there's Claudia. She isn't even pretending to be upset over Andre's death. Elise is grieving far more than she is. What is going on between Claudia and Nick can definitely be called an affair. And it seems pretty obvious that Andre knew what was going on. Maybe he decided to sell the Inn to get Claudia away from Nick. And maybe Claudia killed him so that wouldn't happen."

During dinner, Tempe had told Hutch and Blair how Andre had been poisoned.

"Do you really think Claudia could do something like that?" Hutch asked.

"I don't know what she's capable of. But I do know that when I talked to Nick earlier, he told me that the water from a vase the Lily of the Valley had been in would be enough to kill someone."

"Good Lord."

"Claudia is the one who puts the flowers into the vases. It would have been a simple matter for her to pour the water from one into her husband's pitcher of iced tea." Tempe was quiet for a moment before adding. "Of course it would have been just as simple for anyone else to do the same thing."

"You're right," Hutch said, as he held the back door open for her. Blair had been true to his word, everything had been put away and the kitchen was neat and clean.

Tempe went to the sink and began filling the tea kettle. "Surely Nick wouldn't have told me exactly how Andre was killed if he was the one who did it, or even if he suspected Claudia."

"Not unless he's being extremely clever." Hutch pulled two mugs from the cupboard and set them on the table.

After putting the kettle on the stove, Tempe sat down opposite Hutch. "That just doesn't sound like Nick."

"You've certainly had a busy day. Sounds like you spent most of it investigating the murder."

"By my own choice. Sergeant Guthrie would bawl me out if he knew."

"I know this is something you want to do, enjoy even, but maybe you ought to forget it," Hutch said. "Let the detectives take care of it."

She wondered if he was joking, and searched his face looking for a hint of a smile. When she didn't see one, she said, "But I know all these people. Morrison and Richards don't. They will come up here and poke around, ask a few questions and they'll accept the obvious...that Nick did it. They won't dig any deeper. And they won't come close to finding the real murderer."

Hutch's dimples reappeared, the silver lights sparkling in his gray eyes. "Then I suspect you'd better hurry up and discover just who that might be. I don't want to have to spend our honeymoon here in Bear Creek while you're running around trying to find out who killed

Andre."

Her heart swelled with love. She reached out and took his strong hand in hers. "I promise I won't let anything interfere with our wedding or honeymoon."

"Thank you for the promise, Tempe, but I'm not excited about playing second fiddle to your job though I realize it is inevitable." Hutch continued smiling.

"I warned you," Tempe said.

"Yes, you have. Several times, in fact."

The kettle whistled. Hutch spooned instant coffee into the mugs while Tempe poured the boiling water.

"It's not too late to change your mind, you know."

"I have no intention of changing my mind."

"So have you decided where we're going on our honeymoon?"

"Yes, but I'm not going to tell you, I'm keeping it for a surprise." His grin was surprisingly mischievous.

"But I have to know what kind of clothes to pack."

"I'll tell you that much."

While drinking their coffee Tempe's mind kept drifting back to the murder. Nick's words, "You're going to be real, real sorry you didn't listen", nagged at her, and she wondered if she could be wrong about him.

She thought about Wilbur Carmony and what he'd told her, that the sale and development of the Inn and the surrounding land would only have happened over his dead body. Maybe the dead body he'd been speaking of had been Andre's.

Chapter 10

AFTER HER usual morning jog, Tempe tried to put the murder out of her mind as she began cleaning the house. Wearing jeans, T-shirt and her worn Nikes, her hair in one long braid hanging down her back, she dusted, vacuumed and scrubbed. But she couldn't help wondering if the detectives had arrived in town yet.

By noon, she could no longer control her curiosity. Without changing her clothes, she climbed into the Blazer and headed towards town. When she passed the Inn, she spotted Detective Richards old, faded-blue Ford Fairmont in the parking lot. Knowing she shouldn't, but not being able to help herself, she made a U-turn into the driveway. She parked beside the kitchen door.

Stepping inside, she found Elise, Lupe and two young fellows who worked there regularly. Lupe spotted her first.

"Hi, Deputy Crabtree."

"Hi, Lupe, how're you feeling?"

"Great." She continued rinsing salad greens in the sink.

Elise, who'd been giving directions to the two men, whirled around to face Tempe. Her hair had been brushed straight back and secured at the nape of her neck with a rubber band. Without her elaborate make-up she looked haggard and old.

"What're you doing here again? The detectives just got through with us. We have a restaurant to run, you know."

Tempe made a sweeping gesture with her hands to point out she wasn't in uniform. "I'm not here to ask questions." Thinking quickly, she added, "Hutch and I are having our wedding reception here. I want to talk to Mrs. Donato about that."

"Oooh, Deputy Crabtree," Lupe squealed. "I think it's so romantic you and Pastor Hutchinson are getting married."

"Get back to work, Lupe," Elise scolded. "I suppose Mrs. Donato is free. The detectives left moments ago to look for Nick."

That took care of one of Tempe's questions. "Sorry to have bothered you." She pushed her way through the swinging doors and into the dining room. All the tables had been cleared. The vases had been gathered on a side board, awaiting fresh flowers.

When Tempe reached the door to the office, Claudia stepped out, a basket over her arm, and garden shears in her other hand. "Oh, hello, Tempe. What can I do for you today?"

Tempe decided to continue with the story she'd given Elise. "Last night Hutch told me that he'd asked you if we could have our reception here. I wanted to discuss some of the details with you."

Sounding irritated, Claudia said, "I'm sorry, but after all, I've been busy making plans for my husband's funeral. I haven't had a chance to think about the reception yet."

"Oh, I understand completely. It looks like you were going outside. I'll walk along with you."

"Whatever suits you." With her eyes straight ahead, Claudia marched ahead of Tempe through the kitchen. Elise, Lupe and the young men stared at them with open curiosity.

Even with her high-heeled sandals, Claudia was several inches shorter than Tempe. She walked so quickly Tempe had to hurry to keep up. As soon as Claudia reached the garden, she set her basket on the path. Ignoring the Lily-of-the-Valley, Claudia stepped over to the rose bushes and clipped the stem of a pale lavender bud.

"Pastor Hutchinson assured me that you wouldn't be requiring anything spectacular at the reception. In fact, he told me I could make the decisions as to the buffet and decorations. I suppose now you've got a whole list of demands." She snipped viciously at another stem.

"Goodness, Claudia, nothing could be further from the truth. I'll be happy with anything you decide. I didn't really want a reception."

Claudia placed the rose bud into her basket. She blew a wisp of blonde hair from in front of her light blue eyes and lifted her chin. "Then what was it you wanted to talk to me about?"

"To be perfectly honest, I'm not sure. I guess this whole wedding business has me rattled."

The ruse must have worked because Claudia's expression softened a bit and she shook her head. "You're not kidding, are you? You really don't have a clue. I wouldn't worry about it to much, the pastor told me the women who belong to the chapel are going decorate it, and I'll be taking care of all the arrangements for the reception. All you need to concern yourself with is buying an outfit and doing something with your hair."

Real panic struck Tempe. She hadn't even thought about clothes. "Oh, my goodness. I have no idea what kind of a dress I should wear."

Claudia crossed her arms and rolled her eyes in disbelief. "Really,

Tempe, what kind of a bride-to-be are you?"

"The whole idea is rather frightening. I haven't even thought of myself as a bride."

"It's time you did." She sighed. "After Andre's funeral is out of the way, I suppose I could give you a hand. We can go to Visalia and I'll find you something suitable."

Claudia didn't sound enthused about the idea, and Tempe wasn't sure she wanted to spend that much time with Claudia, but she could certainly use the help. "Thanks, I'd appreciate that."

Tempe could hear someone approaching on the path. Detective Morrison lumbered toward them with Richards right behind.

"Hey, Crabtree, what'cha doing here?" Morrison growled.

Richards squinted as he took in her casual attire. "Not working today?"

"It isn't time yet," Tempe said. "My shift starts at four. I've been talking over my wedding plans with Mrs. Donato. We're having the reception here at the Inn."

"How 'bout that," Morrison said.

"You sure threw Guthrie for a loop when you told him you were getting married," Richards said.

"I hope he's going to give me the time off."

"Said he was." Morrison shifted his bulk uneasily.

"We gotta get on with our investigation." Richards started walking.

"I'll go with you." Tempe smiled at Claudia. "Thanks again. I'll be talking to you later."

Claudia waved impatiently, like she was glad to be rid of Tempe.

In the parking lot, Tempe asked, "So have you found out who killed Donato yet?"

Morrison's prize fighter face displayed relief at the change in the subject. "Like you said, Crabtree, the Indian is the best bet."

"There's plenty of others who had motives and access," Tempe put in quickly.

"Yeah. But this is our case, remember?" Richards whole face squinted at her.

"Oh, sure, I know that. But if there's anything I can do to help..."

Morrison headed for the Fairmont. Before Richards followed him, he said, "You take care of that wedding of yours, Crabtree. We'll manage our investigation."

Frustrated, Tempe watched as Richards backed out of the parking spot and sped through the driveway, spraying gravel. The Fairmont turned right, and Tempe suspected they were returning to Dennison.

Knowing she ought to go back home, she headed toward the Indian path once again. When she reached the garden, she found Claudia in Nick's arms.

"Oops, excuse me again."

Claudia glared at her. "Honestly, Tempe. I thought you left with the detectives."

"I wondered what they had to say to you both."

"I'm not sure that's any of your business," Claudia said.

Two John released Claudia, worry marring his handsome features. "No, it's okay. I have the feeling Tempe's on our side."

"If thinking you didn't have anything to do with Andre's death puts me on your side, Nick, then that's where I am."

"I wish those two detectives felt the same way. It's obvious they're sure I did it. I wouldn't kill another man unless it was the only way to protect my life or someone else's." The Yanduchi crossed his muscular arms and stared stoically off into the distance.

"Can't you do something, Tempe?" Claudia asked as she moved closer to Two John, slipping her hand through the crook of his elbow. He acted as though he didn't notice.

Tempe shrugged. "Everyone keeps reminding me that it isn't my job to investigate Andre's murder."

Claudia looked crestfallen. Two John didn't move or change his expression.

"But I have to confess," Tempe said, "I can't help asking questions and trying to figure out exactly what did happen."

"Thank you," Claudia said, smiling warmly. "I'll appreciate anything you can do to help Nick."

"Finding out who killed Andre is what will help most," Tempe said, "and I'm not sure I'll be able to do that."

Two John shifted his gaze to Tempe's face. "As long as you are certain I didn't do it."

She believed him. But she knew it would take more than her belief in his innocence to keep him out of jail.

REMEMBERING BLAIR'S comment about eating microwaved dinners, Tempe went home and prepared a favorite chicken and noodle casserole for her son before changing into her uniform for work. The school bus dropped Blair off at their driveway just as she was climbing into her Blazer.

"I'm glad I at least got to see you before I left," Tempe said, as

Blair dutifully paused for a hug.

"Anything new with the murder case?" he asked. "All the kids were talking about it at school. Especially since Lupe Madrid was poisoned too."

"Nope. 'Fraid I don't know anything more about the murder than I did when we discussed it last night. I made you something special for dinner. It's in the refrigerator."

Blair swung his pack off his shoulder. "Great. Oh, by the way, the kids were wondering if Lupe and Mr. Donato were both poisoned with the same stuff, how come he died and she didn't?"

That was an easy one but shouldn't be passed along except through official channels. "No one really knows. And if I did, I couldn't tell you yet. All information about the murder has to come from the department. They'll report to the news media anything they want the public to know."

Blair made a face. "Yes, Mother, I'm not a dummy. You've told me enough times. But when the kids brought it up, I wondered about it too."

Of course her son would be intrigued, that was all she'd been talking about lately. She glanced at her watch.

"I wish I could stay home but I can't. Give me a kiss."

He leaned down and brushed his lips against her cheek. She watched as he strode toward the cottage. He turned and waved. After leaving the driveway, Tempe drove to the corner, turned and headed over the bridge that crossed Bear Creek, pausing briefly before pulling out onto the highway.

As was her routine, she drove through town and up past Hutch's ranch. Before she reached the place where she usually turned around, she spotted a car full of teenagers headed toward the high country. Going too fast, the car careened around a curve and crossed the center line. She gave the driver a ticket and a short lecture on the perils of driving recklessly on the winding mountain roads.

She arrived back in town just as some of the businesses closed for the day, though the Inn and the Cafe were just beginning to fill with customers. Tempe parked the Blazer and began a walking tour.

"Hey, Deputy Crabtree," Millie Foster called from the park. She and her three children were taking advantage of the warm May evening. It looked as though they'd purchased dinner from the Cafe and brought it to the park to eat.

"How're you doing, Millie? Kids?"

Millie explained that her husband, Ed, had to work late in

Dennison. Tempe started to walk away as the woman added, "Isn't it terrible about Mr. Donato? Do you think Nick Two John really did it?"

Startled, Tempe paused. "What makes you say that about Two John?"

Hunching her rounded shoulders, Millie raised her hands. "That's what everybody thinks. We all know Nick and Mrs. Donato are lovers."

"No one has been arrested yet," Tempe said. "I think it's a bit soon to be naming the murderer. Enjoy the rest of your evening." To prevent further comments from Millie, Tempe hurried away.

She stopped for a cup of coffee at The Cafe where she faced another barrage of questions about the murder. "Sorry," she pleaded, "I'm not a part of the investigation. I'm afraid I don't know anymore about what's going on than any of you."

The inn seemed to have an unusual number of cars parked along the highway and in the lot for a week night. No doubt some of the customers were thrill seekers, wanting to dine at the scene of a murder. Tempe decided not to make a visit. If Claudia needed her presence she could request it by phone.

When she'd made a complete circle and returned to her Blazer, Tempe decided to cruise the highway. By midnight, she'd handed out three more speeding tickets, and turned a drunk driver over to a highway patrolman.

She stopped for a bar check at the two saloons outside of town, and parked in front of the one in Bear Creek. As she entered, she nearly collided with Edgar Van Tassel.

"Excuse me, Deputy." Alcoholic breath assaulted her. His graying hair needed combing, and his rumpled blue cotton shirt was open at the throat, the tail dangling over the seat of his tan gabardine slacks.

"I hope you aren't planning to drive, Mr. Van Tassel."

A bulbous nose crisscrossed with red and blue veins proclaimed he'd spent many nights in this bar or others. The effort it seemed to take to even keep his heavy-lidded eyes half opened, and the lazy slur to his speech underlined the fact he'd had too much to drink. "Of course I'm planning on driving, how else do you expect me to get home?"

"If you get into your car to drive, Mr. Van Tassel, I'll have to arrest you." She lightly took hold of his arm. "But I'll be glad to drive you home and you can pick up your car in the morning."

Jerking his arm from Tempe's grasp, Van Tassel started to protest, then changed his mind. "Sure, why not. My wife will be mad enough at me as it is."

Tempe opened the passenger door of the cab of the Blazer, he obediently climbed in. When she got in on the other side she saw he was having difficulty with his seat belt and she quickly reached over and fastened it.

As she drove up the highway toward Mr. Van Tassel's saw mill and his home, Tempe said, "I saw the letter you wrote to Andre Donato before he died."

Van Tassel gaped at her. "I didn't kill him."

"What did you mean by 'your life won't be worth a plug nickel'? What were you planning, Van?"

He swiped his fingers through his hair and his left eye began to twitch. "I don't know what I would have done...but I can sure tell you it would have been something if he'd gone ahead with his plans to sell the Inn to Bazmajian."

"Got any ideas who did kill him?"

Tempe knew she shouldn't be questioning the man, but she excused herself because she felt the detectives had already made up their minds.

"There's a bunch of us who weren't about to sit back quietly and let Donato ruin Bear Creek."

"I heard someone wonder why you would mind so much. If the land behind the Inn was cleared wouldn't you be the most likely one to get the trees for your mill?"

"What kind of a person do you think I am, Deputy? For crying out loud, I wouldn't put my business ahead of Bear Creek's welfare. My people been here near as long as yours. Our town is important to me." The man's voice escalated. "No one's going to ruin this place while I still have a breath of life left in me!"

Van Tassel certainly had enough emotion behind a clear motive despite his declaration that he hadn't killed Andre. Tempe wondered if he knew about the poisonous properties in the Lily-of-the-Valley.

"Have you heard what killed Andre?" Tempe asked.

"Poison from some flower, wasn't it? That Indian warned everyone often enough about all the poisonous plants around here, I suppose anyone could have done it."

The tall, cone-shaped building at the saw mill loomed out of the darkness. Stacks of various shapes and sizes of lumber filled the large yard. Tempe drove on past the mill until she came to another opening in the redwood fence that surrounded Van Tassel's property.

The lane looped past a large pond with a rowboat pulled up to a dock. In the back, a redwood house sprawled, floods lighting up the flower gardens and an old fashioned porch stretching across the front. A pale blur of a face appeared in the picture window by the door.

"Damn! Beatrice is still waiting up for me," Van Tassel grumbled. "I'll never hear the end of it."

"Can you make it inside okay?" Tempe asked.

"Could have made it home in my car okay, if you'd let me." The man fumbled with the door before finally swinging it open.

"That's debatable," Tempe said. "Besides, the only options open to you were to let me bring you home, or to be arrested and taken to jail in Dennison."

"Yeah, well, that's why I rode with you." Seeming to be assuring himself of his balance, Van Tassel paused. He took two steps away from the Blazer, before turning back.

Swaying on his feet, he shook a long, skinny forefinger in Tempe's direction. "You want to find out who murdered Donato? You ought to be talking to Wilbur Carmony."

Chapter 11

AN EXPLOSION of wild flowers in a white, yellow, orange, blue and purple abstract design decorated the graves on the hill behind Bear Creek Chapel. The wreaths and potted plants purchased by the mourners and arranged near Andre Donato's final resting place looked cheap by comparison. Pine trees, a few Aspens, along with silver and valley oaks surrounded the cemetery.

Sergeant Guthrie assigned Tempe the task of crowd control at the funeral. At the time, she considered that an unnecessary chore until she'd pulled into the side parking lot of the weathered cedar, A-frame chapel. Even though she'd arrived an hour early, several vehicles were already there. She spotted Hutch's old truck but didn't see him anywhere outside. A couple of saw-horses connected by rope blocked off the area for the hearse and the limousine from the funeral home.

Tempe left the Blazer and headed toward the hill behind the chapel. Several people huddled together near the burial site. Tempe spotted Hutch and Nick Two John standing beneath a large oak shading the newer part of the cemetery.

She ignored the early birds who interrupted their conversation to gape at her with open curiosity. Her dress khakis with the addition of a black arm band and white gloves probably attracted their attention.

As she hiked up the hill toward Hutch who was engrossed in a conversation with Nick Two John, she thought about all the old graves she passed. Most people probably died of natural causes or disease and a few from accidents unlike the man who was about to be buried. Would he find peace while his murderer was still free? Hutch, in a blue clerical robe, was so intent on what he was saying to Two John he didn't notice Tempe's approach. Of course Nick spotted Tempe immediately and watched her progress up the hill.

Two John looked different than usual. Though his long hair was still captured in braids, he'd donned a dark gray pin-striped suit for the solemn occasion.

When Tempe was within hearing distance Two John had returned his attention to Hutch as he said, "Most whites fear death because they view it as an end...a terrifying void. Native people know that their life here is just a part of the journey to the spirit world. In our present life we learn our purpose, what our true work is. Once we make that step over into the other world, our work will continue. Whatever hasn't been learned in this life will be learned there."

The breeze ruffled Hutch's auburn hair, and he still didn't notice Tempe. "H'mmm. What a fascinating idea. But I have to tell you that not all of us feel that death is the end. Christians do believe in a life after death. And though our life's work...whatever that might be...is to be done to the best of our ability and for the glory of God...the Bible says good works aren't the way into Heaven."

"Ah, yes, Heaven. I suspect that's but one of many names for the spirit world. " Two John turned toward Tempe and fixed his deep set, dark eyes upon her. "And what do you think happens when we die?"

Hutch turned, his surprise at seeing her visible on his face. "Tempe, for goodness sake, I didn't even hear you coming." He smiled and opened his arms to her, enfolding her in a hug.

"No wonder. You were so wrapped up in your discussion."

With one arm still around her, Hutch said, "Nick and I have been having the most interesting talk. We'll have to do it again some time."

Nick nodded. "Sure."

Hutch returned his attention to Tempe. "Why the uniform?"

"I'm in charge of crowd control."

Lifting his eyebrows, Hutch repeated in the form of a question, "Crowd control? Really? Claudia told me her husband didn't have any living relatives."

"It's not mourners who will be the problem." Tempe pointed to the small group who'd already arrived. "I don't recognize any of those folks. What I'll have to deal with are the curiosity seekers."

"And it's because of them I didn't wait to come with Claudia," Nick said. "Lupe is riding in the limousine with her. But Claudia wants me to be with her during the service."

"What's the plan, Hutch?" Tempe asked.

"We'll gather at the cemetery gate. I'll escort the widow to the grave site, everyone else can follow. When we've all assembled, the pall bearers will bring the casket up, leaving it next to the grave. Claudia wants it kept simple. There won't be any music. I'll say a few words and close with prayer." More cars had been pulling into the parking lot as Hutch spoke.

"I'd better get down there to keep everyone on the other side of the gate." Tempe said.

While winding her way around the headstones and monuments, she paused beside the group of early birds and asked them to return to the fenced area. They agreed without argument.

By the time the hearse and the limousine pulled into the parking lot, over a hundred people crowded the small area around the fence. About half were Bear Creek residents. Though some of the other faces were familiar, Tempe suspected they had come just because Donato's murder had dominated the front page of the local newspapers and even been mentioned on the evening news of all three major television channels.

Tempe held back the onlookers while Claudia and Lupe were helped from the limousine by the driver. Claudia looked elegant with her blonde hair topped by a black wide brimmed hat with a small veil that dipped over her eyes. A simple black dress showed off her slim figure; her long legs encased in black stockings.

Two John reached her side before Hutch. She leaned heavily on him, as he walked between her and Lupe. A black lace scarf covered Lupe's dark curls. Hutch led them toward the grave site.

When they were nearly half way to the grave, Tempe allowed the rest of the people to spill through the gate. The first ones to rush through were Elise and Wilbur Carmony. Both stared straight ahead as they passed, neither one revealing any emotion.

Van Tassel was the only who hadn't shown up for the funeral. The detectives were the last to begin the climb up the wild flower strewn cemetery hill.

"Crabtree," Morrison said by way of greeting, not turning his battered countenance in her direction.

Richards said nothing at all as he squinted his entire face into what Tempe thought might have been a smile. The pallbearers, whom Tempe later learned were old friends of Donato's from southern California, began the arduous task of carrying the polished oak casket up the hill. She followed them.

Tempe stood away from the crowd, opposite the waiting grave. The casket was lowered onto the lift covered with a blanket of fake grass. Claudia moaned and collapsed against Nick. If he hadn't caught her, she might have fallen to the ground. Lupe gasped.

Hutch raised his hand. "Let us pray. Oh, Lord, we are gathered here together to say goodbye to a man who was a husband, a friend, and a neighbor. We ask that you show Thy mercy upon him as he enters the gates of heaven."

Elise began weeping loudly while her husband looked disgusted.

A couple of men pulled handkerchiefs from their pockets and blew their noses, while several women fished in their purses for tissues.

"Be with those who are mourning his passing, give them the strength they will need to face the void caused by the death of this man. Those of us who know you, thank you Lord, for your blessed assurance that there is life after death. In the name of your Son, our blessed Savior, Amen."

Tempe was surprised by Claudia's weeping. Perhaps her previous uncaring attitude had been caused by the shock of Andre's sudden death. Maybe the reality of her husband's demise had just taken effect. Or maybe she was acting. Perhaps the sudden dramatic display of grief was for the benefit of all those who had gathered for the funeral.

Surprisingly, tears spilled down Lupe's cheeks too. Maybe people cried at funerals because that was what was expected—or maybe it was because thy were reminded of their own losses or immortality.

Hutch kept his head bowed for a few more moments before raising it. "We have gathered here today to say our goodbyes to the earthly remains of Andre Donato. He no longer has any concern for us or for this world. We now must turn our eyes upon those he left behind. Our task, as his friend, is to be there for his widow, to help her through the lonely days and nights to come." He raised his hands. "May the Lord's blessing be with you all."

Some of the mourners filed past the widow to offer sympathy. With his arm around Claudia and his expression somber, Nick soon led the widow back to the limousine. Neither one glanced in Tempe's direction.

"Putting on a good act, aren't they," Morrison growled, startling Tempe. She hadn't noticed the detectives approach.

"If you didn't know better, you'd think the lady is actually sorry her old man was killed." Richards squinted in the direction of the parking lot. "Wonder how hard she'll cry when we arrest her boyfriend."

"Is that what you're planning to do?" Tempe asked.

"Just a matter of time," Morrison said.

Tempe noticed Hutch standing a few feet away. He was probably waiting for her to break away from the detectives. First, she needed to find out something. "Have you talked to Mr. Van Tassel or Wilbur Carmony yet?"

"Nope. And if things keep falling in place the way they have so far, there won't be any need," Richards said.

"I know it's not my investigation..." she began.

"That's exactly right, Crabtree," Morrison put in quickly.

"But I really think you ought to at least interview them. Both men had good reason for wanting Donato dead."

Morrison placed a heavy hand on her shoulder. "Believe it or not, Crabtree, we do know how to conduct a murder investigation."

"I know you do," Tempe said. "But I've had conversations with both those men and what they had to say made we wonder about them."

Morrison's fingers tightened. "No doubt."

"We'll do whatever's necessary, Crabtree. Never fear." Richards strolled away.

Releasing his hold, Morrison said, "We've nearly got it sewn up. Nothing for you to worry about."

She did worry, though, because as she'd feared, the detectives had only investigated the obvious. Nick Two John's involvement with Claudia and his knowledge of the poisonous properties of plants had molded him into the only suspect. Somehow she had to get through to them.

"Hey, wait a minute," she hollered.

Both of the men paused. Richards cast an irritated glance over his shoulder. "Yeah? What is it?"

"Nick Two John didn't poison Andre Donato." Her voice proclaimed the conviction she felt.

With a scowl that made Morrison even uglier, he asked, "Then who did do it?"

"I don't know yet."

Morrison snorted, and both detectives trotted down the hill.

"But I'll find out," she called after them.

Without breaking his pace, Richards turned and shook his finger at her. "Don't go messing around in our investigation, Crabtree. You might foul things up."

Tempe crossed her arms and stared after them.

Hutch moved beside her, putting his arm around her waist. "Might be good advice."

"How can you say that? The idiots are planning on arresting Nick without even questioning any of the others."

Hutch hugged her tighter. "I know you like Nick. But surely they won't arrest him unless they have enough evidence to hold him."

Staring down at the fast emptying parking lot, Tempe said, "They're planning on arresting Nick, I'm sure. But if they do, they won't be arresting the murderer."

"What makes you so positive when everything seems to point to him?"

Tempe turned to face Hutch. "He didn't do it, that's all."

"You must have some reason to think so." Hutch studied her face. She could tell he wanted to understand.

"If he'd wanted to kill Donato he wouldn't have been foolish enough to use poison."

"Actually, it was quite clever," Hutch said. "If Lupe hadn't drunk some of the tea, no one would ever have known Andre was poisoned, and Nick would have gotten away with it."

Hutch was right. It was only because of Lupe's mistake that they even knew the death was murder. Despite that, Tempe was convinced Nick wasn't to blame. "I know he's not the killer."

"You sure are being stubborn about this."

"After all, Hutch, a man's life is at stake. If Richards and Morrison would take the time to ask a few more questions, they'd find out they are wrong."

"Or it could go the other way...add more proof that Nick did it."

"Yes, it could, though I doubt it." Tempe thought Hutch was being every bit as stubborn as she.

His arm still around her waist, he said, "I'll walk you down to your car."

Her mind darted about, wondering how she could make the information she'd discovered about Carmony and Van Tassel available to the detectives. The next time she went to the sub-station she might casually mention it to the Sergeant. Certainly he'd pass it along.

When they reached her Blazer, Hutch took Tempe by the shoulders. "I know you just want to help Nick, but I think it would be better all the way around if you'd just leave matters alone. Let the detectives do their work."

Tempe stared at Hutch. His words irritated her—he sounded just like the Sergeant. To be fair, though, she knew his goal was different. Hutch just wanted her to be unencumbered so nothing would interfere with their wedding plans.

"I'm sorry, Hutch. But if it's possible, I'm going to find out who killed Andre Donato."

"It's so obvious Nick is guilty, I don't know why you can't see it." There was a set to Hutch's jaw and a determination in his eyes Tempe had never seen before.

"I don't want us to fight over this. But whoever killed Andre wanted it to look like Nick did it...and he certainly succeeded."

Hutch shook his head and sighed. "I just don't understand why you keep defending him."

Opening the door of the Blazer, Tempe climbed in. "And I don't understand why you're so darn positive he's guilty."

When Tempe drove out of the parking lot, Hutch stood there staring after her, the blue robe flapping.

Chapter 12

THE PHONE rang just as Tempe reached for the back door knob. It was Hutch.

"Hi, I'm glad I caught you," he said. "I wondered if you'd like to meet me at the cafe for breakfast."

"Oh, I'm sorry. I'd love to, but I'm going shopping with Claudia." After leaving the cemetery the day before, Tempe had gone home. A few minutes previous to the time for her to begin work, Claudia had called, suggesting the shopping trip.

"Really?" Hutch sounded surprised.

"She's helping me find a wedding dress."

"Hey, terrific! Maybe we can get together this evening and you can tell me all about it."

"I have to work, remember? Besides, you aren't supposed to know anything about what I'm wearing until the day of the wedding."

"Maybe we could meet somewhere for your break. We should talk."

"I'd like that." She paused before adding, "I didn't sleep very well last night."

"Me either. That was our first argument."

"I know."

"It's silly for us to fight over something like that...it has nothing to do with us."

Tempe didn't quite agree but there wasn't time to get into it. "I have to go, Hutch. Claudia's waiting for me."

"Have a good time, okay? And sweetheart, I love you."

"I love you too, Hutch." And she truly did, though at times she didn't understand him.

TEMPE DROVE into the parking lot of the inn. Claudia stood beside her Mustang and waved. "I'll drive."

With her bright blonde hair carefully tousled, the short skirt of her teal blue suit revealing her long legs, Claudia didn't look much like someone who was had just buried her husband. Tempe wished she'd asked Claudia what she was planning to wear, but her tweed jacket, brown jeans and T-shirt would just have to do.

Though she would have preferred driving, Tempe parked the Blazer as Claudia slid under the steering wheel of her Mustang. Tempe climbed in beside her. "How're you doing?"

As Claudia started the car and backed out she said, "Everyone asks me that. Why do you want to know?"

Feeling uncomfortable, Tempe shrugged. "You did just lose your husband."

"But it isn't any secret that Andre and I didn't get along. Everyone in Bear Creek knew about Andre and his affairs...and I suppose they all have suspicions about me and Nick."

Tempe felt it best not to comment. Instead she asked, "What are you going to do now?"

"I'm not sure. At first I thought I'd like to move back to southern California but then I'd have to end my relationship with Nick because he would never make it in the big city."

"You're right about that."

"I know. And I can't bear to give him up." Claudia zipped down the two lane highway a few miles above the speed limit. It was a long while before she spoke again. "Before we got married, Andre was the most attentive, loving person. I had my doubts at first, he was so different than any of the other men I'd dated... sophisticated and self-assured."

Claudia maneuvered the Mustang around a truck pulling a horse trailer and didn't resume her dialogue until she'd returned to the right lane. "So many women were chasing him, I thought they might cause a real problem for our relationship. But Andre finally battered down all my doubts and I agreed to marry him. Everything was wonderful for awhile...until he got bored."

Though Claudia drove too fast, she skillfully guided her car around the many curves out of the mountains and into the foothills and around other slower moving vehicles. "It wasn't only our marriage he was bored with, it was everything. The fast pace of our life in southern California, his job, even me."

Claudia took the turnoff to Visalia without slowing, tires squealing. "He began seeing his old girlfriends. I'm sure it wasn't because he was really interested in them, but because of the thrill of doing something he shouldn't."

"A lot of folks are that way," Tempe said. "And its the motive behind many crimes."

"When I found out what he was up to, I told him I was going to leave. He begged for a second chance. Said we'd make a fresh start."

The landscape had become pastoral. Cattle dotted the grass and wildflower carpeted meadows and rolling hills. They passed an occasional ranch house set back from the road.

Claudia continued. "Like a fool, I believed him. He bought the Inn and we moved up here. Though I hated leaving my friends and everything I loved down south, for a short while our marriage did improve.

"Remodeling the Inn fascinated Andre and I soon felt myself being caught up in his enthusiasm. But as time passed and we settled into a routine, Andre's roving eye returned. He flirted with every female who crossed his path. And though I had no proof, I suspected he was bedding Elise on a regular basis." She shivered.

Lupe had corroborated that fact to Tempe.

"That was a terrible blow to my ego since she's so much older than I am. Closer to Andre's age, I suppose, but I certainly couldn't see what attracted him. The challenge, maybe." Claudia applied her brakes to avoid a slow moving tractor on the road in front of her. She poked the nose of the Mustang out several times until it was safe to pass. She didn't speak until she'd settled back into her fast speed.

"One thing I must say, Andre's attention certainly improved Elise. She used to be downright frumpy. Before long, she'd fixed herself up...dyed her hair and had it styled. Even bought some decent clothes."

Tempe had noticed the improvement also, and as she had then, wondered what Elise's husband had thought about the change.

"I didn't care about Andre anymore. In an effort to brighten my dull life, I started looking around. That's when I noticed Nick. He's beautiful. And the opposite of Andre."

Claudia was right about that. She couldn't have picked anyone more different from Andre. Though handsome and masculine, Nick was certainly unsophisticated and unworldly.

"At first I went after Nick only to hurt my husband but it wasn't long before I realized how wonderful he is." Claudia smiled and glanced at Tempe. "I'm sure you don't want to hear all this."

"Actually I'm enjoying it," Tempe said. "I can't remember the last time I had a conversation like this." And there was always the possibility she might learn something that would give her some insight on who had killed Andre and why.

"I can certainly see why you and Nick were attracted to each other," she added to nudge Claudia into revealing more.

Her strategy worked.

"Nick was reluctant, at first," Claudia said. "No matter how much I flirted with him, he didn't react. For awhile I thought he didn't like me, but later I learned he didn't take any action because of guilty feelings." She giggled. "Fortunately, he got over that. You know, Tempe, he's really a wonderful guy."

If Claudia truly loved Nick perhaps she'd killed Andre so her relationship with Nick could be out in the open. And it worked both ways. If Nick felt the same for Claudia, it would have been a simple matter for him to poison Andre.

Claudia interrupted Tempe's thoughts with, "That's enough about me. Tell me how you and Hutch got together."

Once again the scenery changed. They'd driven out of the hills into the flatlands planted with row after row of oranges trees. Tempe told Claudia she'd known Hutch since childhood, but hadn't really paid much attention to him back then.

"It wasn't until I needed his help with a problem that I began to notice him." While they drove through Strathmore, and headed out onto a busier highway, Tempe described how her friendship with Hutch had developed into a romance.

When they finally reached the main thoroughfare through Visalia, Claudia asked, "What kind of dress do you want?"

"I haven't the faintest notion. Nothing real fancy."

"Bridal but not frilly. I know just the place to find it."

Claudia took Tempe to a trendy little shop in a remodeled Victorian home. When Tempe spotted the expensive outfits displayed in the huge entryway, she whispered, "Claudia, are you sure I'm going to be able to afford this? Remember, I'm a single parent living on a deputy sheriff's salary."

"Don't worry." Claudia beamed at the plump middle-aged woman who rose from behind a white French provincial table.

"My dear Mrs. Donato, I was so sorry to hear about your husband." With her round, overly powdered face arranged in a sympathetic facade, the owner of the shop extended both of her hands to grasp Claudia's and kissed an offered cheek.

"Thank you," Claudia said.

"What can I do for you today?"

"Francine, this is my friend, Tempe Crabtree. She needs a wedding dress. She wants something elegant but not traditional. I thought of your shop immediately."

Francine seemed to notice Tempe for the first time. Her

disapproving glance took in Tempe from the single braid hanging down her back to the sneakers on her feet. Once again Tempe wished she'd checked with Claudia about what to wear.

"I have just the style...I only hope I have it in the right size." The woman waddled away from them, her plump hips swaying beneath several layers of the purple cloth she'd wrapped herself in.

Claudia said, "Don't mind her. Trust me, I know she'll have exactly what you want."

Tempe wondered how Claudia could be so positive when she had no idea what that was.

Francine ushered them into a back room which at one time might have been a bedroom. A dainty wallpaper patterned with tiny white rosebuds and pink bows covered the walls. Several mannequins had been outfitted in traditional gowns of satin and lace. An old fashioned free-standing, full-length mirror stood away from the walls lined with rods supporting hangers holding an array of dresses in different lengths and shades of white and ivory.

Tempe's heart beat noticeably faster. With a sure step, Francine snatched a dress from among several. After a quick glance at the tag, she held it up with a flourish. "Were you thinking of something like this?"

The dress was a soft white colored satin, slim but not fitted, with a long sleeved, lace over blouse. Tempe swallowed hard. "It's lovely." She hadn't planned on wearing anything quite so bridal but it was perfect, and she knew Hutch would think so too.

"I'm sure it's your size."

"Try it on," Claudia said. She gestured toward a fabric covered screen.

As Tempe slipped the dress over her head, a startling sensation overcame her. "It's really going to happen," Tempe thought. "I'll soon be a bride." She zipped the back of the dress, smoothed down the sides and stepped around the screen.

"What do you think?"

Claudia tipped her head one way and then the other. "With the proper hairdo and decent pumps, it will be sensational. Take a look for yourself." Claudia turned Tempe toward the mirror.

Tempe gasped. The calf-length dress molded to her figure emphasizing her full bust and small waist. The color complimented the golden tones of her skin and brought out the blue highlights of her black hair. The heart shaped neckline dipped only enough to reveal a shadow of cleavage. She really did look like a bride.

Stepping back in order to see how the skirt hung, she was unable to suppress a giggle when she noticed her scruffy sneakers.

Scowling, Francine asked, "Is there something wrong with the dress?"

"Oh, no," Tempe said quickly, "it's perfect."

"Would you like to try on something else before making up your mind?" Claudia asked.

"Absolutely not. I want this dress. I just hope it isn't too expensive."

Claudia grasped the price tag attached beneath the sleeve and glanced at it. Without changing her expression, she said, "You will be giving my friend the same discount you always give me, of course."

Francine started to protest, but Claudia's compelling gaze stopped her. "Why...ah...indeed."

Even with the discount Tempe thought the price rather steep for a dress she'd only wear once. But she thought of Hutch and how he'd feel when he saw her in it and quickly wrote a check.

AFTER A LEISURELY lunch, Claudia and Tempe headed home. Claudia brought up the subject of her husband's murder. "The detectives have asked me questions three times now, and they've been badgering Nick. Surely they don't think he had anything to do with Andre's death."

Though she knew she shouldn't discuss the investigation with Claudia, Tempe felt obliged to at least comment on her statement. "No one from the sheriff's office has given me an update on what's happening. But I'm sure they are considering Nick as the prime suspect."

"Damn."

"Think about it, Claudia. When you found out your husband had been poisoned, you immediately blamed Nick."

"That was a reflex reaction. As soon as I took the time to consider everything, I knew Nick couldn't have done it."

"Unfortunately the detectives aren't considering everything."

A frown marred her perfectly made-up face, Claudia said, "What do you mean by that? Surely they aren't planning on arresting him?"

"I hope I'm wrong."

With her voice rising, Claudia said, "Tempe, you've got to do something. Please don't let them arrest Nick."

Chapter 13

THE PHONE was ringing when Tempe stepped into her kitchen. It was the dispatcher summoning her to Sergeant Guthrie's office. Tempe's usual routine was to report into the sub-station by telephone or radio, only going in occasionally when transporting a prisoner, to turn in written reports, or when sent for.

Guthrie met her at the door of his office. He made her feel small—one of few men who could—his ruddy face almost purple beneath his salt-and-pepper crew cut. When he didn't say anything about her not being in uniform, Tempe knew she was in store for a lecture.

"I thought I told you to keep your nose out of this murder investigation, Crabtree!"

"Yes, sir, you did."

"Morrison tells me you've been nosing around again."

"It hasn't been exactly like that."

"You haven't been asking questions?"

"Yes, sir, I have. But I haven't been seeking people out in order to do that."

"Well, what have you been doing then?" With his arms crossed, Guthrie continued to block the door of his office. Two male deputies made there way around Tempe, staring with open curiosity. A chubby dispatcher carrying a coffee mug, smiled and patted Tempe's arm as she passed.

"I bumped into someone, or had occasion to talk with a person connected to the case, and the murder has come up. It seemed logical to ask questions. I do have a brain, Sergeant."

Guthrie made no comment but moved out of the doorway. "Come in and sit down. Maybe you'd better tell me exactly what you've learned." He settled behind his desk.

"I think I've found out enough that the detectives should spend more time investigating before they come to any conclusion about who murdered Andre Donato." Tempe pulled a chair directly opposite Guthrie and perched on the edge of it.

He stared at her skeptically. "Okay. So tell me."

"First there's the matter of how Donato died." She catalogued how easy it would have been for anyone to have poured the water from one of the vases that held a Lily of the Valley into Donato's special tea.

"Yeah, and the obvious one was Two John."

"It could have been Mrs. Donato. She's the one who put the flowers into those vases."

"You think she killed her husband?"

Tempe shook her head. "Not really. Nearly everybody in Bear Creek knew about the poisonous properties of the plants because of Two John's guided nature walk, just as they knew about Donato's special tea. And the kitchen was always open. Anyone could have walked in and doctored the tea when no one was around."

The Sergeant leaned forward. "According to the detectives, Two John is the one with the best motive. Screwing around with the man's wife and wanting to prevent the Inn from being sold so he wouldn't lose his job."

Yet another motive was what the developer planned to do to the environment, but Tempe kept quiet about that. "There were others who were just as unhappy about the Inn being sold." She reminded him of the threat in Van Tassel's letter, and told him when she'd discussed the letter with the him, she learned there were others who were just as determined not to let Donato ruin Bear Creek.

"So you think Van Tassel is a suspect?"

"One of several."

"You have any real evidence pointing to Van Tassel?"

She wondered what he thought she'd just been telling him. "And then there's Wilbur Carmony."

"Who is Carmony? I don't think I've heard about him."

"Wilbur Carmony is Elise's husband."

The Sergeant sighed and raised a shaggy, gray eyebrow.

Tempe described the relationship between Elise and the murder victim ending with, "It wasn't exactly an affair. Everyone seems to think Donato was taking advantage of Elsie...even Wilbur."

"How come you know all this?"

"Everyone in Bear Creek is talking about it."

"Sounds like a soap opera. But I don't see that you've got any real evidence on any of those folks."

Exasperated, Tempe stood up. "No, I don't. But it does seem to me that all of them ought to be questioned by the detectives. It's their job to dig up the evidence. You've certainly reminded me of that often enough. All those people had as much of a motive to kill Donato as Nick Two John."

"Morrison and Richards feel they have enough against Two John to convict him. They plan to arrest him some time today." Guthrie rolled his chair back and stood.

"Damn. How can you let them do that? Didn't what I just told you mean anything?"

"I'm only in charge of this substation, Crabtree. But the detectives report to the D.A. who is also convinced of Two John's guilt. I'll pass along your information to him, but I don't think it's going to make any difference."

That left Tempe with no choice. She'd have to continue the investigation on her own. "If there's nothing else..."

"Still want that time off?" he asked.

His question took her by surprise. "Ah, yes, of course I do."

"You can have the last two weeks of June."

She frowned, that didn't give her much time.

"Something wrong with that?"

She shook her head. "No, that's fine."

"I expected a little more gratitude." Guthrie scowled. "I had to convince someone with a lot more seniority than you to change his vacation plans to accommodate yours."

"That's great. I appreciate it, truly I do."

"Good. I'll be expecting an invitation to the wedding."

"You'll have one," Tempe said, hoping she'd remember. She hadn't even considered things like wedding invitations. All she had on her mind was how she should go about finding out who killed Andre Donato.

When she arrived back in town, she spotted Hutch's truck parked outside the cafe. Like the Inn, the cafe had been around as long as she could remember. She decided to stop and give him the news about the time off.

She immediately spotted Hutch's slightly mussed, deep auburn hair as he sat alone at one of the booths that lined the narrow interior. He wore his usual outfit of plaid shirt with sleeves rolled up to his elbows, well-worn Levis, and scuffed-toed boots making him look far more like a cowboy than a preacher.

A grin lighted his face as soon as he spotted her, and he jumped to his feet. "This is great! I hoped I'd see you sometime today."

He gripped her in a bear hug, and Tempe inhaled his clean scent, a combination of soap and the outdoors.

After a kiss that didn't last as long as she would have liked, he released her and she slid into the Naugahyde seat that had been repaired in several places with different colored tape. The café looked like a log cabin on the outside. The inside had seen few changes over the years except for new blue-and-white gingham curtains at the windows.

"I'm having a late lunch, what can I get for you?"

"I'd love a hamburger," she said.

Hutch went up to the counter and gave her order. When he returned, he reached across the Formica table top and squeezed her hand. "Did you find a dress?"

"Oh, yes. And you're going to love it."

"I'm sure I will." His gray blue eyes displayed his adoration for her. "Did you and Claudia have a good time together?"

She nodded. "Actually it was fun." She gave him a brief description of their shopping spree. "And I have some terrific news."

"Tell me."

"I just came back from the sub-station. Sergeant Guthrie's given me the last two weeks in June for my vacation."

"Fantastic! Now we can really move ahead with our plans." Hutch's broadly grin deepened his dimples. He caressed her cheek.

His gentle but sensuous touch made her eager for the honeymoon.

Hutch asked, "Did you and Claudia discuss the reception?"

"She's going to take care of it."

"I thought I'd ask Blair to be my best man."

"Oh, Hutch, that's so sweet. He'll be tickled."

"Well, I don't know if that's quite the reaction I had in mind." His eyes twinkled.

The waitress arrived with their food. She exchanged pleasantries while placing it in front of them. When she'd gone Tempe started unwrapping her hamburger.

Realizing Hutch was staring at her, she asked, "What is it? Is something the matter?"

"That's what I was going to ask you. I have this feeling there's something else you haven't told me."

"How do you do that? I wasn't going to say anything until later."

His dimples disappeared. "I knew it. You don't seem to have your heart in our wedding plans."

Tempe took a deep breath. "The Sergeant gave me some other news that isn't so good."

"About the murder case, I suppose."

"Yes, they're planning on arresting Nick sometime this

afternoon."

Hutch looked relieved. "You have been expecting that, haven't you?"

"I guess so. But it really upsets me that they haven't taken the time to investigate any of the others."

"Obviously they feel they have the right man."

Tempe nodded. "Obviously. But they're wrong."

With his voice low, Hutch said, "Maybe you are, Tempe. Everything points to him being the murderer."

"It's possible, of course. But I just don't think so."

"You're usually so objective about everything, I don't understand why you aren't in this case. Is it because Nick is an Indian?"

"What would that have to do with anything?"

"Maybe you're more sympathetic toward him because of your mutual heritage."

"For goodness sake, Hutch, that's not got anything to do with it. They've got the wrong man."

Hutch smiled again. "Okay, sweetheart, you're probably right. Sorry I said anything. Why don't we change the subject and enjoy our lunch."

"Good idea." Tempe took a bite of her hamburger but she wondered why Hutch had become so adamant about Nick's guilt. And this new business he'd thrown at her about not being objective because of their mutual Indian heritage, where had that come from?

Chapter 14

TEMPE LEFT a note on the dryer for Blair. "Sorry, no time to cook. Microwave leftover macaroni and cheese tonight. Love, Mom." After leaving Hutch, she had only enough time to shower and don her uniform. She'd hoped to see Blair before leaving the house, but the school bus was late. Tomorrow was Saturday, they'd at least have the morning to be together unless he'd made other plans.

Along with her discomfort over Hutch's uncharacteristic lack of sympathy toward Nick Two John, she was unhappy about not being more involved in Blair's life. But that wasn't anything new. The shift she worked didn't give her much time for the men in her life.

She began work by patrolling the campground at the lake. A toddler, nothing on but a diaper, waved at Tempe as she passed an umbrella tent and a picnic table covered with a red-and-white checkered cloth. The mother, a stocky tanned blonde, scooped the child into her arms and smiled. The father didn't look up. He was busy building a fire in a cement ring.

Except for several older couples who relaxed in lounge chairs beside their expensive motor homes and trailers, most of the weekend residents were families. She didn't see anyone who might cause problems later in the evening.

She drove back onto the highway, stopping to issue a speeding ticket. Because it was Friday, she knew traffic would increase between Dennison and Bear Creek and the other campgrounds higher in the mountains.

A minor accident at the edge of town drew her attention, and after she'd written her report she was called to investigate the burglary of a new, large home used only on weekends by a wealthy couple from southern California.

While she worked, she kept wondering if Nick had been arrested yet. She suppressed her curiosity until nearly eleven when she spotted Lupe crossing the almost empty parking lot of the inn.

"Hey, Lupe," Tempe called, as she parked the Blazer near the beginning of the Indian trail. "How're you doing?"

Lupe appeared surprised to see Tempe. "I'm okay, Deputy Crabtree."

Tempe climbed out of her vehicle. "What's new?" If Nick had been arrested, surely Lupe would know.

The girl shrugged. "Nothing much. Had a big dinner crowd."

"That's good, isn't it?"

"Sure." Lupe stared at Tempe thoughtfully and ran her fingers through her curly dark hair. "I've been meaning to talk to you about something."

"Really? What?"

Lupe glanced around. "Not here, someone might be listening. Let's go up the trail a bit."

Though the lights from the parking lot didn't extend far into the gardens, Lupe walked surefooted ahead of Tempe. Tempe wished she'd brought her flashlight as they hurried past the herb and flower gardens and black silhouettes of the trees against the indigo sky.

Lupe didn't stop until she reached the meadow and the fork in the trail. "There's something I should have told you."

"What is it, Lupe?" Tempe asked. The darkness obscured the girl's expression.

Once again, the atmosphere felt menacing. Ominous shadows obscured everything around them. Lupe moved closer to Tempe.

"I wish I didn't have to mention this, but I haven't been able to sleep."

"What is it, Lupe?"

A twig snapped down the trail. Lupe jumped. Tempe wondered if someone had followed them. She took Lupe's arm. "We should find a more private place to talk."

"We can go to my cabin."

Four simple box-shaped buildings loomed out of the darkness when the path Lupe had taken opened onto a clearing. Lupe pointed to the nearest, the only one with a light on inside. "This one's mine."

A tiny porch with a railing held a reed rocking chair and a full Boston fern planted in a terra cotta pot. Lupe pushed open the unlocked front door and smiled. "Welcome to my home."

A pot-bellied stove, a white wicker couch and chair, a flat-topped wicker trunk and a square wooden table and two straight backed chairs crowded the tiny living room and kitchen combination.

"You did a good job decorating," Tempe complimented, taking in the bright patterned pillows, the crocheted Afghan, the potted plants that sat on every available surface along with family photographs. A curtained alcove led into what Tempe guessed was the bedroom, and there were two closed doors near the kitchen area—bathroom and storage maybe.

"Thank you. Sit down, please." Lupe sat at one end of the small couch, Tempe on the other. She waited expectantly.

"I really like Nick Two John," the girl began.

"Yes, so do I. What you have to tell me is about Nick?"

Lupe bowed her head and picked at her fingernails. "I didn't mean to eavesdrop, but I was setting the tables in the dining room and the door to the office was open. They didn't know anyone was around. I should have made more noise to let them know I was there."

"We've all been in awkward situations like that, Lupe."

A smile briefly lifted the corners of her lips before she continued. "Mrs. Donato told Nick that her husband hit her. Nick sounded real mad about it."

"Then what happened?"

"Mrs. Donato asked Nick to kill her husband."

Tempe felt sick. "What did he say?"

"His first words were muffled. But then I heard very clearly, 'simple matter. No one will ever find out.'"

"Those were his exact words?"

"Yes, I'm sure."

"I'll have to report that, Lupe."

"I know. But what's going to happen to Nick?" Her concern was apparent in her dark eyes.

"He'll be charged with murder. Frankly, I expected him to already be arrested by this time."

"The detectives were here earlier, but Nick hasn't been around. He took off sometime after his nature walk and he hadn't come back by the time I got off work. Mrs. Donato kept coming into the kitchen asking if any of us had seen him."

Tempe hoped he hadn't decided to run. No doubt Claudia had told him what Tempe had said on the way home from their shopping excursion, and he knew he was the prime suspect. Smart as Nick was, the news probably hadn't been any surprise to him.

"Is there anything else?" Tempe asked.

Lupe shook her head.

Rising, Tempe said, "I've got to go. The detectives will want to hear about this from you."

She nodded and stood beside Tempe. "Can you find your way back by yourself?"

"I think so. It's just a matter of following the trail."

"Thank you for listening, Deputy Crabtree."

After stepping outside the comforting glow from Lupe's cabin, Tempe again wished for her flashlight. She kept her eyes on the path in front of her so she wouldn't stumble, but she soon became aware of the noises coming from the woods around her. Twigs snapped, leaves rustled, night birds cried out, frogs croaked, and crickets chirped.

Though the sounds she'd heard many times before, in the dark on the unfamiliar path they unnerved her. Moving as quickly as possible without running, Tempe came to the meadow. Knowing she didn't have much farther to go, the tension left her.

Without warning, Nick leaped out in front of her, blocking her way. A tiny squeak of surprise escaped Tempe's lips. "Oh my goodness, Nick, you startled me!"

With his fists on his hips, his legs spread, Two John glowered at her. "Where have you been?"

"It really isn't any of your business, Nick." Tempe kept the panic she felt out of her voice.

"You've been to Lupe's." He said. "What did she tell you?"

"I'm sorry, Nick." She tried to push past him but he wouldn't move out of the way. The thought struck her that maybe everyone else was right about Nick, and she was wrong.

"I'm sorry we never had a chance to really talk, Tempe. There's so much I could have shared with you." He continued to block her way.

"Like what?" Tempe wondered if she was going to hear a confession, and if she were in any danger. She rested her hand on top of her holster.

"There are so many things you're missing out on. You've never heard the Yanduchi legends." A cloud moved from in front of the half moon, a muted ray of silver dusted Two John's neatly parted hair. With his braids framing his high cheek boned, chiseled face, Tempe imagined Nick in Indian garments and moccasins.

"You've never even sung our songs. Poor Tempe, you're merely the shell of a Yanduchi."

She did not speak. Any distraction might prevent him from revealing his true motive for stopping her.

"Becoming a true Yanduchi isn't something that can happen overnight. I could have been your guide."

Tempe wondered why he used the past tense. Did he expect something to happen to him? Or was something about to happen to her? A shiver of fear scooted down her back bone.

"I'm sure it would have been a fascinating experience," she said, attempting to squeeze by him. "You'll have to excuse me, Nick, I must get back to work."

He grasped her shoulders, preventing her from moving. Not releasing his hold, he continued speaking as though he'd not been interrupted. "You could have learned the secrets of our people. Carefully guarded secrets. And once you learned these things, the mysteries of life would begin to unfold before you." Nick glowered fiercely at her.

In an attempt to break the spell he'd cast, Tempe said flippantly, "The only mystery I have to solve right now is how to get away from you."

Nick snatched his hands away as though he'd been burned. His intense expression disappeared like a mask dropping off. "I never intended you any harm, Tempe." But he continued to block her way.

"I know that, Nick." And she did.

"I have great sorrow for you. You have missed so much because of the denial of your heritage."

"I haven't denied my heritage," she protested.

"Oh, but you have. Your denial is expressed by your ignorance."

Tempe's fear shifted to annoyance. "This has all been most interesting, Nick, but I'm on duty right now. I've gotta get going. So if you don't mind..."

He turned sideways, allowing her to pass. "I'll go with you. It is time."

She didn't know what he meant, but she wasn't about to ask. "Suit yourself." And she wasn't going to discuss with him what Lupe had told her, especially not while they were alone.

Tempe hurried down the trail, conscious of Nick following right behind her. She wondered how he'd managed to evade the detectives, and if he'd done it on purpose or if they'd just missed him somehow.

After passing the herb and flower gardens once again, she stepped out into the lighted parking lot. Morrison and Richards stood beside her Blazer.

Morrison moved toward her. "Thanks for bringing Two John in."

"But I..." Tempe turned toward Nick. "I didn't know. I'm sorry."

"But I did," Nick said.

Richards squinted at Nick. "Put your hands on the hood of the car and spread your legs, Two John."

While Morrison patted him down, Richards recited his rights.

The kitchen's screen door banged open and Claudia burst out.

"What's going on out here?"

As soon as she spotted Nick being handcuffed, she started running across the parking lot, her high heels making staccato sounds on the asphalt. "Oh, my God, Nick! What are they doing to you?"

Chapter 15

CLAUDIA, ARMS open wide, ran toward Nick but she was blocked by Morrison's muscular bulk. "Stay back, ma'am."

Tears began streaming down Claudia's face. "Please, don't do this."

"We've just arrested this man for your husband's murder," Richards said as though that might change Claudia's attitude.

"He didn't kill Andre. You've got the wrong person," Claudia wailed.

"We don't think so, ma'am," Morrison said, and continued to obstruct her while Richards led Two John toward his car.

"Don't worry, Nick. I'll get you out," Claudia gasped through her tears. "I'll hire the best lawyers."

Nick didn't look back as the detectives' car took him away.

Tempe held her arms out to Claudia planning to console her. With smudged mascara, Claudia's eyes reflected hatred. "This is your doing, isn't it, Tempe? You've been pretending to be my friend in order to trap Nick."

Taking a step toward her, Tempe said, "No, no, that isn't the way it was at all. I even talked to my Sergeant this afternoon about the case. Told him I didn't think Nick killed Andre..."

"Liar!" Claudia shouted.

As long as she was already mad, Tempe decided to bring up the subject Lupe had talked to her about. "Tonight I heard that you asked Nick to kill Andre. Is it true?"

Claudia gasped. "Who told you?"

"That isn't important, but your answer to my question is."

"This is all your fault. You led the detectives right to Nick. They could have never found him without your help."

"No, Claudia, that's not what happened. I had no idea the detectives were out here waiting for Nick. But I think he knew...and that he was ready."

"Nonsense! I've had enough of this conversation...and I've had enough of you, Deputy Crabtree." Claudia stamped her heel. "You aren't welcome around here anymore. But don't worry, I'll do your reception for Pastor Hutchinson's sake."

Tempe opened her mouth but before she could say anything, Claudia had spun around and stomped off toward the inn. Feeling frustrated by the evening's events, Tempe hoped that by morning, Claudia might realize she was not responsible for Nick's arrest.

She glanced at her watch, and sighed. Time to get back out on the road. It was pretty quiet for a Friday night, she hadn't had many calls. She moved the Blazer in front of the bar, and stepped inside. The long narrow room buzzed with lively conversation. Blue smoke hovered near the ceiling and in the shadowed corners of the darkened room.

"Deputy Crabtree." The bartender acknowledged her as he filled a glass from the beer tap.

"How're things going?" she asked, glancing down the bar. It held the usual array of cowboys and other locals. The several tables were occupied by couples. A few of the customers nodded or smiled, though most were so engrossed in their own conversations they didn't notice her.

"Quiet crowd. Everyone's happy," the bartender said.

Tempe smiled, that was what he always told her. "Glad to hear it."

She was just about to leave when Clay Warner, one of the cowboys, slid off his bar stool. "Hey, Deputy, wasn't that Nick Two John I saw in the back of that unmarked police car just a bit ago?"

All the faces at the near end of the bar turned curiously in her direction. "I'm afraid so," she said. There was no reason to deny it, the news would be around town before the afternoon paper was delivered.

"He did it, huh? Two John poisoned Donato." Pleasure radiated from Warner's weathered and bushy mustache decorated moon face.

"Remember, he's innocent until proven guilty." Tempe backed toward the open door, not wanting to discuss the case.

Wilbur Carmony staggered out of the smoky shadows. "Indian did us all a big favor. Ought to take up a collection for him. Deserves a reward." His words were slurred.

"Sounds like it's time you headed home," Tempe said.

He ignored her. "There isn't anyone in this town that isn't glad Donato's dead. Deserved what he got." Wilbur hitched up his pants, sweat glistened on his bald head. "Had no respect for anyone."

She couldn't leave Wilbur in the bar in his condition, and he certainly couldn't drive himself home. But before she could say anything else, Wilbur's lower lip began to quiver, and his eyes filled with tears. His shoulders shook and he started to cry.

"Hey, Carmony, what's the matter?" Warner asked, frowning.

"Ruined her...that's what he did...ruined her," Wilbur gasped between great sobs.

"Who're you talking about, anyway?"

Everyone in the bar had focused on the dramatic scene though Carmony was unaware of his audience.

"Elise...my wife...most wonderful woman on earth...'til he got hold of her...filled her head with lies...poisoning was too good for him." He sobbed even louder, burying his face in his hands.

"He needs to go home," Tempe said.

Warner slung his arm around Carmony's shoulder. "I'll tend to him."

"Thanks." Tempe followed as Warner led the still sobbing Carmony outside. When she climbed into the Blazer, Carmony was handing the keys of his black truck over to Warner. Good.

Tempe drove through town. So much had been going on she'd like to discuss with Hutch. She drove past the fire station on the right, and the inn on the left. Her thoughts went to Claudia. Sadness settled over her, sadness because of the loss of the newly formed friendship with Claudia and sadness for Two John. Despite Tempe had heard from Lupe, she still couldn't believe that Nick was responsible for Andre's death. And when she reported what Lupe had told her, the information certainly wasn't going to help Nick.

Despite all the evidence accumulated against Two John, Tempe remained convinced that someone else was the murderer. Because no one except Claudia agreed with her, it was left to Tempe to prove Nick's innocence. But how on earth was she going to do that?

Before she realized it, she had driven the two miles past Bear Creek Chapel to the entrance of Hutch's ranch. She slowed the Blazer and turned the steering wheel. She followed the winding lane down toward Hutch's two-story, gray house snuggled beneath the mountains in a broad valley.

When she pulled up in front of the old house, she realized that all the windows were dark. Of course Hutch was already in bed, it was after one. She really wanted to talk to him. There was so much she needed to sort out. But then she remembered their last two meetings and his unexpected attitude about Nick's guilt along with his surprising accusation that she couldn't be objective about Nick.

She put her forehead against the steering wheel and closed her eyes. Hutch had always been so supportive before, she just couldn't understand what was going on.

A few days ago, if she'd been as troubled about something as she was now, she wouldn't have hesitated about waking Hutch to talk to him. He would have welcomed her warmly. But she was afraid he wouldn't be so receptive tonight because she wanted to discuss how to prove Two John's innocence.

Raising her head, she pushed the gear shift into reverse and backed around. As she drove up the lane, she realized how tired she was. It was time to go home and to bed.

In the morning, she reluctantly called in to report the conversation between Claudia and Two John overheard by Lupe. Because it was Saturday, she knew nothing much would be happening with the case. Two John was safely incarcerated, while Guthrie and the detectives enjoyed their weekend.

Though she didn't have much of an appetite, she prepared Blair's favorite breakfast, pancakes and sausages. The tantalizing odor brought her sleepy-eyed son into the kitchen. He hadn't combed his corn silk hair, and he still wore the Raiders T-shirt and the brightly colored baggy shorts he'd slept in.

"Hi, Mom." He kissed her and settled in his usual place. "Breakfast looks great." He slathered his stack of pancakes with butter and poured on the syrup.

Tempe sat across from him and sipped her coffee. "What are your plans for the day?"

He pointed to his full mouth. After swallowing, he said, "Got to finish my term paper for Smith's class. Don't have too much more to do, but it'll probably take the rest of the day."

Blair put down his fork and stared at her. A line appeared between his blond eyebrows. "Is something wrong? You look kind of strange."

Tempe smiled at him. "Yeah, maybe. But it isn't anything to concern you. Eat your breakfast."

"Don't worry, I won't let any of it go to waste. But why don't you tell me what's happening?" He resumed shoveling food into his mouth.

"A problem has come up between Hutch and me."

Blair registered surprise. "Oh, yeah? I thought you guys were pretty tight. This isn't something that's going to affect the wedding is it? I've been looking forward to having another man around the house."

"I hope not."

"So what is it?" He speared another sausage and put it on his plate.

"Nick Two John was arrested last night for the murder of Andre Donato."

"That isn't any big surprise, is it? Everyone at school has been expecting that to happen."

"I don't think he did it."

Blair poured a glass of milk and downed half of it before he said, "Why not?"

"Nothing concrete. But it seems to me if Nick had been the murderer, he wouldn't have left so many clues pointing to him."

"What's this got to do with you and Hutch?"

"Hutch is just as convinced of Nick's guilt. When I try to talk to Hutch about why I think Nick is innocent, he starts acting funny. He even accused me of not being objective because Nick and I are both Indians. Isn't that crazy? I just don't understand where that's all coming from."

It started as a snicker, growing quickly into a belly laugh. Blair whooped and hollered until tears filled his eyes.

His reaction startled Tempe, and puzzled her. "I don't see what's so funny."

"Oh, Mom, he's right about you not being objective, or you'd have figured out the problem right off the bat. Hutch is jealous of Nick Two John."

"What? That's the most ridiculous comment I've ever heard. Hutch has absolutely no reason to be jealous of Nick."

Blair shrugged. "Since when is jealousy reasonable?"

"Hutch isn't like that."

"Maybe not usually. Stuff like this happens all the time at school. I bet I'm right about him."

Tempe still couldn't perceive why Hutch would be jealous of Nick Two John. She shook her head.

"Think about it, Mom. That Two John guy is a real stud. And he's kind of been coming on to you."

"Oh, he has not!" She felt her face warm from the embarrassment she felt.

"Sure he has," Blair said. He waved his fork in her direction. "He might not have meant anything by it, but you're a fine looking woman...and still single for a little while longer. Fair game."

"Oh, I can't believe it."

"Believe it. I bet that's exactly what's got Hutch uptight."

Of all the foolish reasons to be upset. Tempe knew she'd never led Nick on, and if, as Blair put it, he had been coming on to her, she truly hadn't recognized it.

"I don't think Nick has that kind of interest in me at all, Blair,"

Tempe said. "He loves Claudia Donato. He just enjoys bugging me about not knowing anything about the Yanduchi culture."

"You could be right about his attention being innocent. But obviously, it doesn't look that way to Hutch. And when you keep defending Two John, it probably makes Hutch think you're attracted to the guy. Makes sense, doesn't it?"

Tempe nodded. Actually, it was beginning to. She hugged Blair. "You've grown up while I wasn't looking. How'd you ever get so smart?"

"Like I told you, we talk about this kind of stuff a lot at school." Blair wiped his plate with the last of his pancakes and popped them into his mouth.

"You do?" She was amazed that she knew so little about her son.

"Oh, sure. Relationships and all that."

"I can see we really need to be spending more time together. Do you have a relationship with someone?"

"I don't have a special girl right now, if that's what you mean. But I'm good friends with plenty."

Oh my. Of course there were lots of girls, Blair was a good-looking young man. She felt the need of Hutch's steady guidance in their home all the more.

Blair started laughing again.

"What's so funny now?" she asked.

"You should see your face, Mom. Don't you think I'm old enough to have a girl?"

"Of course you're old enough. I was just thinking how much I need Hutch around here."

Blair stood, stretching out his long, lanky frame. "You need Hutch all right, but not because of me. I think you ought to go talk to him."

"Now?"

"The sooner the better. You guys should get all this stuff out in the open."

Tempe knew her son was right. She considered calling Hutch to tell him she was coming but decided against it. She knew he'd be at the chapel working on his sermon, surprising him might be best.

Chapter 16

TEMPE HAD made up her mind to surprise Hutch, she decided not to change clothes. If she did anything to put off going she might reconsider. Besides, Hutch was used to seeing her in jeans and a pullover. If she dressed up, it might put him on guard making it even more difficult to bring up the subject she knew they must discuss.

His truck was parked beside the church. The front door was unlocked and she stepped into the sanctuary. The morning sun poured through the stained glass window near the ceiling on the front wall, splashing multi-colored rays over the neat rows of polished oak pews.

Tempe hurried to the door leading to Hutch's office. It stood ajar. She knocked lightly as she pushed it open. "I hope I'm not interrupting."

Hutch glanced up from the papers and books scattered over the slab table set upon two-drawer filing cabinets that served as his desk. "Tempe! For goodness sake. What brings you here?" He grinned, quickly sweeping his glasses off, laying them down on his open Bible. "What a wonderful surprise!"

"We need to talk."

Shoving his swivel chair back, Hutch stood and hurried toward her. A line creased his brow. "Is something wrong?" He opened his arms to her and kissed her.

Tempe returned his kiss and hugged him tightly, drawing comfort and strength from the nearness of his body.

When she pulled away from him, Hutch kept his arms around her. "What is it?"

"Nick Two John was arrested last night."

His gray eyes shadowed briefly. "You knew it was only a matter of time. Sit down, Tempe. Tell me about it." He led her to the worn faded blue couch in front of his desk and sat beside her.

"There's much more. Claudia blames me for his arrest. We were both in the parking lot of the inn when he was picked up."

"She has to strike out at someone, you were convenient."

"We were just getting acquainted. It isn't easy to make friends...or keep them...with my job."

"No one knows that better than I do," Hutch said. "But I'm sure once Claudia has time to think, she'll come around. I'll talk to her, if you'd like."

Tempe shook her head. "There's more. I visited with Lupe Madrid last night and found out something unsettling. She overheard Claudia ask Nick to kill her husband."

Hutch sat up straight and tilted his head. "Did he agree to do it?"

"Lupe couldn't hear everything he said, but what she did hear was 'It's a simple matter'...and...'no one will ever find out.'"

Relaxing against the back of the couch, Hutch said, "Now I guess you're ready to accept Nick's guilt."

Tempe ignored Hutch's comment. "I spent some time with him just before he was arrested."

The same strange shadow clouded Hutch's eyes. "Oh? And what was that about?"

Blair's assessment was correct. Hutch was jealous of Two John. "He talked to me about what it means to be a Yanduchi."

Hutch said nothing.

She continued. "He spoke about how he could have taught me the spiritual side of being a Yanduchi. But everything he said to me was in the past tense. It was like he knew he was going to be arrested. He even said, 'It is time' right before we stepped out where the detectives waited for him."

In a controlled voice, Hutch asked, "How did you feel about that?"

"Terribly sorry for him because I know he didn't kill Andre."

"How can you still believe that after what Lupe told you?"

She could sense the tension like a barrier between them. Tempe grasped his hands. "My darling Hutch, before I came to see you, Blair and I had an interesting discussion. He thinks you might be jealous of Two John."

"Jealous! Of all the ridiculous...sounds like a sixteen-year-old kid's fool idea. Why on earth should I be jealous?"

Though he tried to pull his hands free, Tempe clung to them. She stared into his eyes. "That's just it, sweetheart, you have absolutely no reason to be jealous of Nick. My only interest in him is merely the fact that he is the prime suspect in Andre Donato's death."

"You keep standing up for him when it's so obvious he's guilty," Hutch snapped.

Tempe smiled at him. "There's no reason why we can't have

differing opinions on the subject, but did you hear how you said that?"

Hutch blinked. He was quiet for a moment. Speaking slowly, he said, "You and Nick share something that I can never be a part of. Perhaps I am jealous."

"Of my Indian ancestry. I have to admit, Nick has certainly raised my curiosity about it. Even more so last night."

Hutch lowered his head. "Do you want to tell me more about last night?" He added quickly, "You don't have to, if you don't want to."

"Of course I want to, that's the main reason I came. It seems to help to talk things over with you."

"I'm glad."

"I was coming back from talking to Lupe in her cabin, when Nick stopped me on the trail. He startled me and at first I felt threatened. I wondered if everyone else had been right about him, and I was wrong. But as he talked, a strange sensation came over me. It was as though we'd stepped back in time." She thought about how she'd imagined Nick dressed in Indian garments.

"What all did he say?"

"How I wasn't a true Yanduchi because I didn't know the songs and secrets of our people. He said he could have been my guide, that he would have helped me to understand life's mysteries."

"Sounds like he was trying to convert you," Hutch said with a hint of annoyance.

"Not really, because he spoke like it was too late for me to embrace the Yanduchi beliefs."

"And why was that?"

"He said it was because I denied my heritage through my ignorance. But that wasn't the only reason."

"Oh? And what else was there?"

"It was something that I sensed. It was if he knew something was about to happen to him, that he wouldn't be around to serve as my guide. Right after that he was arrested."

"If he killed Andre, he would expect to be caught," Hutch said.

"Yes, that's true. But while Claudia and I were shopping, I told her Nick was the prime suspect."

"And of course she told him."

"I'm sure of it. So if he'd chosen to, he could have continued to elude the detectives like he'd done earlier in the day. If Nick had wanted to keep from being arrested he would have disappeared."

Hutch was silent for a moment. "You sound like you think Nick has supernatural powers." Irritation had crept into his voice again.

"No, Hutch, that's not what I think at all. But I do know he is very clever about some things. Things that have to do with him being a Native American."

The frown had returned to Hutch's face. Tempe smiled. "In case you don't realize, you have many attributes I admire much more than any of Nick's cleverness."

The frown deepened until Tempe leaned closer and brushed her lips against his. "I love the way you stand firm in your beliefs, how you truly care about everyone, and go out of your way to help folks. You always listen to me. You're a good friend to Blair." She smoothed a fallen lock from his forehead. "I love everything about you...but most of all, how you show me in so many ways how much you love me."

"Oh, Tempe, I wasn't...surely you don't think...I didn't mean..." Hutch paused. A huge grin spread across his face, his dimples creasing his cheeks. "Listen to me! I can't believe I'm responding this way! Maybe I really do have a problem with Nick Two John. I'm going to have to pray about it."

Tempe caressed his face. "Actually, it's rather flattering that you have these feelings. But you shouldn't be jealous. It's you I love. I'm marrying you."

He brushed a wisp of black hair away from her cheek, his hand sliding down until it cradled her neck. "I love you so much. I'm counting the days until we're married." He pulled her against him again, his lips sought hers.

Tempe could feel his heart pounding against her breast as they kissed, while her own heart seemed to swell with the love she felt for him. Being in his arms pushed all thought of the murder investigation away. While tasting his sweetness, she ran her fingers through his thick, auburn hair, and inhaled the scent of his spicy aftershave mixed with his clean, masculine aroma.

His lips slid from her mouth to her ear. He whispered, "Tempe...Tempe...Tempe..." his warm breath tantalizing, and his caresses becoming more insistent.

"No, my darling. Not here."

"I don't care where we are. I can't wait any longer, I need you, Tempe. I want you now."

There was nothing Tempe longed for more than to have Hutch make love to her—however, his office in the church wasn't the place she'd had in mind. For the first time, she was the one to pull away from him.

Straightening her clothes, she said, "This is difficult for both of us." Kissing him quickly, she pulled away. "I have to go now."

"Tempe, no, please..."

"You know I can't stay."

Hutch, his skin flushed beneath the freckles, sighed as he finger combed his hair. "I suppose you're going right back to investigating the murder."

Tempe stood up. "Of course I am, Hutch. I have to keep trying to find out who killed Andre."

Hutch nodded. "Forgive me, Tempe. I wouldn't expect anything less from you. I don't know what's the matter with me, I'm certainly not behaving like myself."

Glancing from beneath her lashes, she said, "I'd like to think it's because you're so much in love you just can't control yourself."

"That's true." Hutch clasped her hands. "You are driving me crazy. I feel like a schoolboy."

She gestured toward his desk. "It looks like you have plenty to keep you busy."

"It's awfully hard to concentrate when all I want to do is make love to you." He peered at her so wistfully, Tempe wished she could just forget all about the murder and the chores she needed to do at home, and spend the rest of her time before work with Hutch.

Instead, she blew him a kiss and stepped out of the room.

BLAIR LOOKED up from his history books and the papers scattered on the kitchen table as Tempe opened the back door. "How'd it go?"

"Great. And I thank you for the suggestion," Tempe said.

A satisfied grin spread across her son's face. "Glad to help."

She spent the rest of her time at home straightening the house and doing the laundry, while she planned her strategy for trying to discover Andre Donato's murderer and clearing Nick Two John of the crime. Re-questioning anyone who might have had anything to do with Donato's death or had a motive would be a priority. She'd like to question Claudia further, especially about the conversation Lupe had overheard, but she didn't think Claudia would talk to her.

Nick might be more willing to open up to her now—especially after spending the night in jail.

Tempe decided to get ready for work early, and go down to the sub-station to interview Nick. It would be a good time since the Sergeant wouldn't be around to interfere.

Blair put the finishing touches on his term paper and picked up his books by the time Tempe had prepared a late lunch of fried chicken and potato salad.

While they shared the meal, Tempe asked, "What're your plans for tonight?"

"Going to the movies with some of the guys," he said as he picked up his third piece of chicken.

"Don't stay out too late."

"Mom!" Blair rolled his eyes.

"I just thought it would be nice if you'd go to church with me in the morning. I know Hutch would be pleased to see you. We might even eat together afterward."

"Anything to help the cause."

"Good. How about cleaning the kitchen for me, I'm going to get ready for work now."

"Isn't it kind of early?"

"I've got to go to Dennison." Blair didn't need to know why she was going there.

TWO JOHN was surprised to see her. Tempe took him from the small holding cell into an interrogation room. "Take a seat, Nick." She sat opposite him on the other side of a scarred table.

"What brings you here? Is there some news?" he asked eagerly.

"Nothing good, I'm afraid. I wanted to talk to you about my visit with Lupe last night."

Nick didn't say anything, he just stared at her, his black eyes piercing.

"Lupe told me about a conversation she overheard between you and Claudia."

Without blinking or moving, Nick waited.

"She heard Claudia asking you to kill Andre."

With no emotion in his voice, Nick said, "That was right after Andre hit her."

"Lupe said she couldn't understand everything you said. But she did hear you say, 'It's a simple matter' and 'no one will ever find out'." Tempe watched Nick carefully for a change of expression.

He crossed his muscular arms before speaking. "Too bad she couldn't hear it all."

"Why don't you tell me what it was?"

"Will it make a difference? Everyone is so sure I killed Donato, nothing I say in my defense is going to matter."

"I don't think you did it."

Nick's deep set eyes widened slightly, his straight black eyebrows raised, and he lifted his chin. "How come?"

"If you killed Andre, you wouldn't have left so many clues pointing in your direction."

"That's absolutely right. If I had put the poison in Donato's drink, as soon as he had his first glass full, I would have seen to it that there was no chance for anyone else to get into it. If Lupe hadn't gotten sick from drinking that tea, no one would ever have known the man was murdered."

"True. Dr. McClatchey was satisfied Andre had died of natural causes until Lupe was brought into the hospital. He ordered Donato's autopsy after that. So tell me what Lupe didn't hear."

With his back straight, his long braids hanging over his shoulders, Nick began. "It wasn't the first time Donato had struck Claudia. He'd slapped her around before...but this time he really hurt her. She was desperate when she asked me to kill him. If she'd had a weapon, I think she might have done it herself."

Tempe had always known Claudia could be a suspect. Nick must have guessed what she was thinking because he quickly added, "She hated Nick and she was afraid of him...but she didn't kill him."

"I want to hear exactly what you said after she asked you to do it."

"I did say it would be simple to do. But I also said I couldn't kill a man under those circumstances even though there were ways it could be done so that no would could ever find out."

If Nick was telling the truth, Lupe just hadn't heard his complete answer to Claudia. Tempe believed him.

"Nick, I can't make any promises about your freedom, but I will do all I can to find out who did kill Andre."

Two John smiled for the first time. "I know you will...and I appreciate it."

"I wish I didn't have to take you back to that cell."

"Don't concern yourself. Though my physical being is locked behind bars, nothing can contain my soul."

As Tempe opened the door, Two John said, "Tell Claudia I'm doing fine, that she needn't worry."

"I'll try, but she's not very happy with me right now. Blames me for your arrest."

Walking ahead of her down the corridor toward the holding cell, Two John said, "She's quick to anger and quick to forgive."

During the drive back to Bear Creek, Tempe reviewed her list of suspects. She was absolutely convinced of Two John's innocence, and nearly as sure Claudia hadn't been responsible for her husband's death.

But as in the case of Nick, Tempe had no proof, it was merely a feeling. She hadn't even heard Claudia's say that she hadn't killed her husband. Maybe Claudia was the next person Tempe should confront.

Chapter 17

TEMPE STEPPED through the front door of the inn. Dressed in a gown of soft, flowing pale blue, her blonde hair casually tousled, Claudia had stationed herself at the desk just inside the entrance to greet her customers. Her smile immediately turned into a frown.

Clicking her long, pink fingernails against the stack of menus atop the desk, she asked, "What brings you here, Deputy? Obviously you're on duty since you're in uniform."

"I went to see Nick this afternoon, and he gave me a message for you," Tempe said.

Claudia's expression softened immediately. "Really? How is he?"

"He looks good. Can we talk privately somewhere for a few minutes?"

"Can't you just tell me what he had to say? This is our busiest night, you know," Claudia snapped.

"It won't take long, but it would be better if we weren't interrupted."

"Oh, I suppose. Just let me get Lupe to take over here."

Claudia ushered Tempe into her office and closed the door, but she didn't sit behind her desk, nor did she offer Tempe a chair. "Go ahead."

"Nick wants you to know that he's doing fine and that you shouldn't worry about him."

"Hah! How can I help but worry. They won't let me bail him out until after the arraignment, and that isn't until Monday morning. He won't be able to stand being locked up like that."

Tempe thought of the many times Two John had been incarcerated during his alcoholic past. "He seems to be handling it all right. Said nothing can contain his soul."

Claudia smiled wistfully. "That sounds like Nick."

"I have a couple of questions for you, Claudia."

She sighed and glanced at her watch. "Hurry, please."

"Did you kill your husband?"

"I was wondering how long it would take you to ask. The answer is no. I'm sure I don't have to tell you there was no love between us. If he'd lived, I planned to divorce him...but I didn't kill him."

"Someone overheard you asking Nick to kill Andre."

Claudia glared. "What busy-body did that?"

"It doesn't matter who, I just want to know if that's true."

"Oh, it's true all right, but didn't whoever told you this also tell you that Nick refused to do it?"

"Unfortunately, the person couldn't hear that part. But I questioned Nick about the incident, and he told me everything he said. But the detectives will know about it on Monday, and it isn't going to help Nick's case."

"Damn!"

"Claudia, when Nick refused you, did you ask anyone else to kill your husband?"

"Absolutely not! I wouldn't have said such a ghastly thing to Nick if I'd been thinking straight at the time. I was just so angry with Andre..."

"Angry enough to want him dead?"

"Yes, I admit it. At the time I most certainly was. But neither Nick nor I had anything to do with his murder."

"Do you have any ideas about who it might have been?"

"Not really. Like I told you before, there were plenty of people around here who didn't like him very much...nor what he had planned for Bear Creek."

Tempe knew that was true. The task she'd assigned herself to uncover Nick Donato's killer seemed impossible.

"Is that all? I really need to get back out there."

"Claudia, listen to me for a second. I'm positive they've arrested the wrong man for Andre's murder. But the detectives on the case are just as sure Nick did it, and all the evidence points to him. There's only one way to help him, and that's to find the guilty one."

Claudia's eyes and mouth opened wide. "But I thought you were responsible for Nick's arrest."

"Yes, I know. But it doesn't matter. What does matter is that the real murderer is found. If you think of anything at all, please, call the station and tell them you need to talk to me. Will you do that?"

"Oh, Tempe, I'm so sorry. I thought you were a traitor." Claudia threw her arms around Tempe and hugged her. She was smiling and tears glistened in her eyes when she pulled away. "I'd like to help you. There's nothing I want more than for Nick's innocence to be proven. But, honestly, I just don't have an inkling who did it."

A striking change came over Claudia as she returned to her hostessing duties. She held her head higher, her eyes sparkled and her smile had brightened. Tempe feared she'd given Claudia false hope. Tempe certainly didn't feel terribly optimistic about her chances of solving the case. Perhaps the mere fact that she was willing to try had been enough to lift Claudia's spirits.

Since she was at the Inn, Tempe decided she might as well stop in the kitchen and question Elise. The restaurant usually drew a crowd on Saturday night, and as Tempe passed through the large room she didn't notice a single empty table. Lupe, along with two more waitresses, were taking orders and delivering round trays crowded with dome-topped platters to the diners.

Tempe stepped out of the way of one of the new waitresses pushing through the swinging doors, and she followed behind. Pots simmered on the big stainless steel stove, steaks and seafood sizzled on the grill, two men dressed in white aprons and armed with long forks and spatulas, poked and stirred.

Other kitchen helpers bustled about, putting together salads and filling plates. A dark blue apron protected Elise Carmony's neat white blouse and tailored blue skirt. Her hair was brushed tightly back into a bun, and her face was devoid of make-up. Elise had total control of the action, like a conductor over an orchestra.

When Elise noticed Tempe, she frowned. "Is something wrong, Deputy Crabtree?"

"No, Mrs. Carmony. I only want to ask you a few questions."

Everyone had paused, openly staring with curiosity at their boss and Tempe.

"Don't cook that steak too long, Julius," Elise snapped. "Get back to work, everyone." She glared until the clatter had increased, and all were busily engaged in their tasks. "This isn't a very good time, can't you see I'm busy?"

"I won't bother you long. I just wondered if on the day or evening before Mr. Donato died if you noticed anyone in the kitchen who didn't belong here." Tempe backed out of the path of another waitress.

Elise rolled her slightly protruding eyes and crossed her arms over her plump chest. "The only ones I can think of are you, your son, and Pastor Hutchinson."

"Think about it for a bit. You just might remember. Someone who didn't have any business in the kitchen."

"People are always traipsing through who don't have any business here." She stared pointedly at Tempe. "What's this all about anyway? I heard Nick Two John was arrested last night."

"I'm not convinced he's the one who killed Andre," Tempe said.

Elise blinked. "Well...who else could it have been?"

"I don't know, that's why I'm asking questions."

"I'm sorry, but I don't remember anything unusual about the day Andre was murdered and I really must get back to work." She turned away from Tempe.

"Please, Mrs. Carmony. Take some time to think about it a little more. I'll come back later when you aren't so busy."

Elise scowled. "Whatever suits you, but I really don't have anything more to say." Tempe noticed that the cooks and the other kitchen helpers glanced in her direction with unhappy expressions, too. She wasn't sure if that was because of the fact that she had interrupted or because they feared Elise.

Disappointed, Tempe left through the back screen door. She'd talked to three people already and knew no more than she had before. Proving Nick innocent would be even more difficult than she imagined.

She walked through the crowded parking lot. If Claudia kept the restaurant, it didn't look like she'd have any problem making a living with it. Her husband's murder seemed to have drawn even more customers to the already popular eating place.

When she neared the Blazer parked out in front, she spotted Edgar Van Tassel helping his very stout wife into their perfectly maintained, older model Cadillac. "Mr. Van Tassel, wait a minute. I'd like to talk to you."

Van Tassel tucked his wife's skirt inside the car and slammed the door before straightening up to greet Tempe. "Deputy Crabtree, what can I do for you?"

"Wonder if I might ask you a few questions?"

The tall man leaned against the passenger door, crossing his arms, his keys dangling from a finger.

Mrs. Van Tassel rolled down the window, and though Tempe couldn't see her because her husband blocked the way, she could hear his wife very well. "Edgar, what's the problem? What are you standing out there for? I'm ready to go home."

"Hush, Beatrice. The deputy wants to talk to me."

"What for? Did you do something wrong? Carousing around again, I bet. When are you ever going to grow up."

"I said that's enough, Beatrice." He spoke sharply, and the window closed again.

"I won't keep you long," Tempe said. A breeze blew down from the mountains, cooling the warm evening air.

"Good, Beatrice doesn't have much patience."

"You've heard about Two John's arrest, I suppose."

"That's all anyone can talk about it seems."

"I don't think they've arrested the right person."

Van Tassel's left eye began to twitch. "Oh, yeah? You know something the rest of us don't?"

"Not really. What were you doing the day Andre Donato died."

"What the hell is this, Crabtree? You don't think I had anything to do with..."

The Cadillac's window rolled down again. "What's the matter, Edgar? Why are you yelling?"

"Stay out of it, Beatrice. Shut the window." He spoke fiercely, and the window was quickly closed.

"I'm just trying to eliminate suspects..." Tempe began.

"Suspects!" Van Tassel roared. "I'm a suspect?"

"I saw that threatening letter you wrote to Donato, remember?"

"That's all it was...just a threat. I was trying to make sure he didn't sell the Inn and the land around it to that damned developer." Van Tassel dropped his hands to his sides, seeming to shrink an inch or two.

"But the last time I talked to you, you made it quite clear that if Donato had gone ahead with his plans that you most certainly would have done something to prevent it. How do I know that isn't exactly what happened?"

The twitch in his eye became more noticeable. "I didn't kill Donato. And to answer your question about where I was that day, I was at the saw mill as I am every weekday. I went home for lunch, and after work, that's where I went again. We had company over for dinner that night, I think. You can ask the misses, she'll tell you." He knelt down and knocked on the glass of the window.

The window came down and Van Tassel stepped aside. His wife poked her puffy face, with its several chins and nearly hidden eyes, out the window. The wind blew her halo of pale pink curls. "What on earth is the problem, Edgar? Are we ever going to be able to leave?"

"Deputy Crabtree wants to know what we were doing the night Andre Donato died," Van Tassel said.

"Why on earth would she care about that?" Mrs. Van Tassel asked.

"Just answer the question, Beatrice," he snapped.

His wife's face reddened beneath the dusting of powder. "You know what we were doing as well as I do, why didn't you just tell her?"

Van Tassel's voice grew louder. "Beatrice!"

"We had a dinner party that night. Would you like a copy of the guest list?"

"That won't be necessary," Tempe said. "What I would like to do though, is stop by the saw mill and talk to your employees about your comings and goings on that day."

"Why on earth do you need to know that? What's the reason?" Mrs. Van Tassel's voice rose shrilly. "You can't possibly think...Oh, my God! Edgar, what have you done? I knew your foul temper would get you in trouble..."

"Shut up for Pete's sake, Beatrice! Please!" His loud command finally silenced her. Like a turtle withdrawing into its shell, her head disappeared inside the car.

"You can come by the saw mill anytime, but you aren't going to find out anything that will link me to Donato's murder. You'd be better served to talk to Wilbur Carmony like I told you to before."

"Why do you say that, Mr. Van Tassel? What about Mr. Carmony?" Tempe had already planned to question Carmony next.

"Get your answers from him. I'm not going to pass along gossip about my friends."

Tempe didn't think Van Tassel and Wilbur Carmony were such good friends. Of course they were acquainted, everyone in Bear Creek knew each other, the two men even drank in the same bar. But the couples didn't socialize. Van Tassel had been a friend of Donato's before the question of the sale of the Inn had arisen. But Tempe knew Beatrice Van Tassel would never have counted Elise Carmony among her chums, since Elise was an employee of the Donatos.

"You can go now, Mr. Van Tassel. I'll probably be around to talk to your men sometime Monday."

"Do what you want, Deputy." Van Tassel stomped around his Cadillac and jerked open the door.

Tempe headed toward her Blazer. She wondered where she could find Wilbur, and if he'd be as angry with her questioning as Van Tassel had been. So far her investigation hadn't turned up anything she didn't already know. But her time was limited. Once Sergeant Guthrie found out what she was doing, he'd make her stop.

Despite her promise to Van Tassel, she'd probably only have the weekend to find out who killed Donato. That wasn't enough time.

Chapter 18

"WHAT THE hell are you doing here?" Wilbur Carmony peered at her from the two inch gap of his opened front door.

Tempe had searched for him around town with no success, finally deciding to try his home a few miles outside of Bear Creek. The Carmonys owned a double-wide mobile home atop a wooded knoll. At the back and to the side, a large barn dwarfed the house.

"I'd like to talk to you about Andre Donato's murder."

"No comment."

"You've had plenty to say the other times I've talked to you."

"Yeah...well...that's all there is." He started to shut the door but Tempe leaned against it, keeping it open.

"I've got a few questions about some of your previous remarks."

"Tough shit."

There was no way Tempe could force the man to talk to her. But she decided to thrust right into his most vulnerable spot. "I'd like to know how you felt about your wife's relationship with Donato."

Carmony shrank away from the door. A worn bathrobe swung open over the pale concave chest and pot-belly which hung over the waist of his faded jeans. His feet were bare.

Tempe stepped inside, Carmony pulled his bathrobe together and collapsed onto the end of a flowered velvet couch. The bald, untidy man seemed strangely out of place in the crowded room with its matching beige-and-brown plush furniture, artificial flower arrangements and ceramic figurines crammed onto every available surface. Most of the light came from the flickering images on the television though there were plenty of lamps with ruffled shades that he hadn't bothered to turn on.

"What's this all about?" he grumbled.

Though she hadn't been invited to sit, Tempe perched on the edge of one of the chairs nearest her reluctant host. "You've mentioned several times that you aren't the least bit sorry about Andre Donato's death."

"No law against being honest."

"And is that because of your wife's relationship with him?"

Carmony sat up straight, his reddish face deepening to scarlet. "I already told you it didn't amount to a hill of beans."

"That's not what you said the last time I saw you, Wilbur."

"Oh yeah? When was that?"

"Last night."

"I don't remember seeing you last night."

"That's because you were drunk. I was in the bar when Clay Warner had to take you home."

"Oh." Carmony squinted and his head began to bob. Tempe suspected his memory was clearing.

"What you said was that Elise had been the most wonderful woman in the world until Donato got hold of her and filled her full of lies. What kind of lies were those, Wilbur?"

Carmony lifted his moon-face in Tempe's direction. "None of your business."

"I'd like to make that decision for myself," Tempe said.

"Doesn't concern you, Deputy, not one little bit."

Knowing she'd have to jog Carmony to get him to say anything incriminating, Tempe said, "Quite a few folks have already told me your wife was having an affair with Donato."

"That's not the way it was at all," Carmony snarled. "Far too many busy bodies in this town."

"Then why don't you explain to me how it was, Wilbur?"

Carmony was silent for such a long time, Tempe wondered if he was ever going to answer. When she thought she might have to prod him once again to get him to speak, he finally began.

"Andre Donato was a no-good, lying, defiler of womanhood. Turned my Elise's head with nonsense and phony flattery. She never even looked at another man in all the years of our marriage until Donato came along."

"How did you find out about Elise and Andre?" Tempe asked.

"Knew something was going on when Elise started making herself up like some kind of floozy. Dyed her hair, even. Made her look like a cheap, middle-aged tramp. Told her so too. She started coming home from work later and later with all kinds of feeble excuses. Went down there one night to see what was keeping her. Peeked through the kitchen window and spotted that sneaky weasel sucking on my wife's neck, his hands all over her." Carmony made a sour face at the memory.

"So what did you do?"

"Went back home, acted the way I always did. Figured somewhere down the line, that pole cat would show his true colors and Elsie would come to her senses."

"You didn't confront either of them about what you saw?" Tempe found it hard to believe the blustery man could have kept such a secret.

"Nope. Wasn't any need. Knew he didn't want my wife on a permanent basis...why would he? Had that pretty little woman of his own. Figured before long Elise would discover he'd been playing her for a fool."

"Is that what happened?" Tempe asked. "Or did you get tired of waiting?"

Carmony jumped to his feet. "What're you trying to do here, Missy? You accusing me of something? It wasn't me that did Donato in, not that I wouldn't have liked to. But if I'd killed him, I'd have wrung his scrawny neck with my bare hands." Once again Carmony's complexion reddened as he leaned over Tempe.

Tempe slid out of the chair to stand eye to eye with him. "What about Elise? Now that Donato's dead did you tell her that you knew about her affair with Andre?"

Carmony pushed his nose within inches of Tempe's, and she could smell his sour breath as he said, "Get this straight, Deputy, there wasn't any affair. Donato sweet- talked my wife into his bed and tossed her aside when he was done with her."

"How do you know that, Wilbur? Is that what Elise told you?"

Carmony cinched the sash of his robe tighter. "That's all. You don't need to know anymore. Donato's dead, the killer's locked up. All the rest is best forgot. It's time my life got back to normal."

"I wish it could be that easy," Tempe said, as she headed for the door. With her hand on the knob, she paused and turned. "The problem is, I don't think Nick Two John murdered Donato."

"That's a mighty big problem 'cause you're wrong. He's the only one could have done it."

Despite Carmony's words, Tempe had the distinct impression there was far more about his wife's affair and his reaction to it than he'd revealed. She had to learn the complete truth before she could solve the mystery surrounding Donato's death.

On her way back into town, Tempe stopped a speeder and gave him a ticket. She reached the inn just in time to see Wilbur Carmony's truck turn into the parking lot. She parked the Blazer long enough to watch Carmony, a plaid shirt replacing his bathrobe and boots covering his bare feet, leap from his truck and dash into the kitchen.

Tempe decided to follow him when her radio crackled to life.. "Large animal reported blocking the road near the intersection of Fern and Cedar."

No matter how much she wanted to know what prompted Carmony to visit his wife, the dispatch had priority. Fern and Cedar came together near the highway. If the large animal was a bear or stray cow, it might cause an accident. If it was a deer, it would be gone long before she reached the location.

It turned out to be a cow. She recognized the brand on its rump, and had the dispatcher call the ranch. She remained with the animal to alert traffic to the hazard until a cowboy arrived and loaded it into a trailer. The incident took about forty-five minutes. Though she knew Wilbur had plenty of time to take care of his business, she decided to stop back by the inn. Maybe Elise would have time for her now— maybe she'd even want to talk to her after Wilbur's hasty visit.

The inn's parking lot had emptied considerably. She looked around as she entered. Wilbur's truck was gone, and so was Elise's car. Except for the kitchen and a few of the upstairs' windows, the building was dark.

Inside, the only ones still working were Lupe, the other waitresses, and the kitchen helpers. The cooks were finished for the evening, and Elise Carmony was nowhere in sight. Lupe glanced up from pulling plates out of the dishwasher. "Deputy Crabtree, is something wrong?"

"No, no. I wanted to see Mrs. Carmony. I had an appointment with her this evening."

Lupe piled the clean plates atop a stack on the drain board. "Gee, I guess she forgot. Her husband stopped by a while ago. He must've told her something important, cause she was sure in a big hurry to get out of here."

"I see." He told her something important all right, he told her about Tempe's visit. For some reason, maybe Elise didn't want to talk to her after hearing Wilbur's version of their conversation. Maybe the revelation of Elise's affair with Andre was too embarrassing—but Tempe thought it probably was more than that. Elise didn't seem the type to allow embarrassment to get in her way.

"Did she say where they were going?" Tempe asked.

Lupe shrugged. "Mrs. Carmony didn't say anything to me except she had to leave. She didn't even tell me to clean up...which isn't like her at all. Whatever was going on must've been serious."

Tempe agreed and wished she knew what it was.

SHE DROVE BY the Carmony's mobile home—neither of their vehicles were visible and the house was dark. Though she thought it likely the car and truck had been tucked away in the barn, she doubted if the Carmonys would respond to her knocking. Though Elise's and Wilbur's actions were suspicious, they didn't constitute any real evidence of complicity in the murder. Tempe felt discouraged. It didn't look like she was going to be able to help Two John's situation at all.

Her first reaction to her frustration was to seek out Hutch, but she decided against it. Though Hutch had admitted his jealousy of Two John was unfounded, revealing that she was feeling blue because of not being able to find any real evidence against someone other than Two John might resurrect emotions in Hutch she didn't have the energy or the time to deal with.

The only other person who could raise her spirits just by the sight of him was Blair. She wondered if he'd gotten home from the movies yet and decided to drive by and check.

Weak color glowing through one of the front windows of her cottage meant the TV was on, a sure sign of Blair's presence. She parked the Blazer and hurried inside. "Hey, Blair!" she hollered, rushing through the kitchen and into the hall.

With a puzzled expression, her son poked his blond head around the doorjamb of the living room. "What're you doing home so soon?"

"Just thought I'd stop in and check on you."

Blair rolled his eyes.

"Actually, I was feeling kind of down. Seeing you has perked me up already." She reached over and patted his cheek.

"It's a good thing you did stop by. I have a message for you."

"Really? What is it?" She couldn't imagine who it could be...everyone knew she worked evenings. The best way for anyone to get in touch with her was through the substation. The dispatcher relayed all such messages by radio.

"Lupe Madrid."

"When did she call?"

"It's been awhile. She sounded funny...scared maybe. She was whispering like she thought someone might hear."

"What did she want?" Tempe didn't know whether to be alarmed or prepare herself for a joke, he was drawing the information out so.

"She just said for you to come to her cabin at midnight."

"Tonight?" She still wondered if she was being set up.

"That's what I asked, but she just said, 'uh huh' and hung up."

Tempe stared at him, waiting for the punch line.

"I think you better go, Mom, she didn't sound like herself."

"This isn't a joke?"

Blair made a face. "Of course it's not a joke. What did you think, I was making it up or something?"

Tempe shrugged. "Sorry, but it sounds so mysterious. Can you remember when she called?"

"Not exactly...a few minutes after I got home, I think. After ten."

Around the time she saw Lupe at the inn—whatever the problem was must have come up soon after she left.

"Give your mother a kiss, sweetie, I've got to get back to work."

Blair dutifully leaned over and kissed her. He said, "You are going to see Lupe, aren't you?"

"Of course, I am. I can't imagine why she'd want to meet with me at such a late hour but it does make me all the more curious."

"I'm going to bed. There's nothing interesting on television and I haven't forgotten my promise to go to church with you in the morning."

"You're a good son, Blair."

"And you're a good mother. Be careful, okay?"

"Always am." On the way to her Blazer she glanced at her watch, wouldn't be long before the time Lupe had designated.Tempe hoped the girl hadn't come up with some more incriminating evidence about Two John that she'd tardily decided to confess. Whatever it was, Lupe must think it important enough to arrange such a mysterious meeting. Tempe couldn't stop wondering about it as she toured the nearly deserted roads of Bear Creek.

Chapter 19

ALL THE WINDOWS in the inn were dark, even those in Claudia's quarters. Clouds blown by the wind intermittently covered the moon. Tempe pulled her flashlight from its holder under the dash; she wasn't going to find herself wandering around out in the dark without it again.

No sooner had she stepped on the Indian trail when the sense of dread she'd experienced in the past settled over her. As soon as she followed the path into the gardens where the parking lot lights no longer reached, she switched on her flashlight. Only a small orange circle appeared in front of her, the battery was low.

"Darn!" Hopefully it would last until she reached Lupe's cabin.

She concentrated on the walkway in front of her as it wound through the beds of flowers and herbs. Though she didn't look up she was acutely aware of the thick growth of vines and trees just beyond the carefully tended gardens.

The night sounds seemed magnified. The wind rattled the leaves and sent dust and debris flying. Something crashed through the underbrush, startling Tempe. Probably a deer. But the unexpected noise had caused her heart to beat faster, and she stepped up her pace. Without conscious effort, she strained her ears for the many sounds surrounding her.

An owl hooted, bats swooped across her way. A twig snapped, followed by the sound of another. Could someone be following her? Tempe paused and listened.

She heard nothing but the usual nightly orchestra of frogs, night birds and insects with the background of the wind whooshing through the forest.

As she continued onward, a stealthy footfall sounded somewhere behind her. Once again she halted, listening. But she could discern nothing unusual. She turned slowly, aiming her feeble flashlight beam along the path she'd just taken. The pale orange circle turned the wind-animated plants into strange animals, the bushes and trees beyond into grotesque monsters. But she couldn't pick out anyone or anything that shouldn't be there. She chided herself for her overactive imagination.

What was there about the Indian trail that threatened her? She'd spent many nights tramping about in the dark elsewhere, searching for a burglar or fugitive, and never before had she experienced such a sense of foreboding. It was as though the trail was haunted, inhabited by malevolent spirits. She smiled at her bizarre thoughts.

If Two John were here he'd undoubtedly assure her that only helpful spirits of their ancestors would be astir on his Indian trail. And if Hutch were along, she wouldn't be afraid at all.

She reached the meadow where the trail divided, and quickened her step as she headed toward the cabins. A movement to the side caught her eye, just as she heard the unmistakable sound of heavy steps just behind her. But before she could turn, something crashed down on her head. Pain exploded into a million shards hurtling her into the black hole of unconsciousness.

THE ENTIRE BACK of her head radiated excruciating throbs. For a moment she had no idea where she was. Slowly she opened her eyes, and she knew she was sprawled right where she'd been attacked. With her fingertips she tentatively examined the spot where the pain originated, she felt warm stickiness—blood.

She tried to look around without moving her head in case her assailant was still around. There was no way of knowing how long she'd been out, though the night seemed as dark and oppressive as before. Perhaps even darker; clouds hid the stars from view.

Knowing she at least needed first aid, Tempe tried to raise her head. Blackness closed in on her. She fought to stay conscious. When her head cleared, she scooted her knees and arms under her, until she was able to raise herself to a kneeling position. Using her hand for support, she stood slowly, fighting dizziness.

Taking a step, her toe kicked against something metal—her flashlight. With great care, she squatted to retrieve it. But when she tried the switch, she realized it was on but the battery was completely dead. Like her attacker had meant for her to be.

It was closer to Lupe's than returning to the Blazer. Maybe she should radio in her predicament before going any farther. Automatically she reached toward her belt, the radio was gone! Quickly she felt for her holster. Empty! Though she knew she'd been left for dead, her assailant had made sure if she did survive, she couldn't call for help or protect herself.

Hurrying as fast as she could without jarring her head, and trying to be alert to a possible second attack, Tempe made her way down the winding trail. When she finally reached the clearing, she was surprised to see Lupe's cabin was dark. She had to be there. Why would she ask for Tempe to come if she wasn't planning on staying home to meet her?

Maybe Tempe had been out so long Lupe got tired of waiting, thought she wasn't coming and had gone to bed.

No longer worrying about whether someone might be lurking in the shadows, Tempe darted toward Lupe's porch. Her head ached even more.

She knocked sharply on the door. At first there was no sound from inside the cabin.

She pounded with her fist. Someone padded across the floor, a frightened voice asked, "Who's out there?"

"Deputy Crabtree. Let me in."

The sound of a chain being slid open was followed by that of a simple lock being turned. Lupe opened the door.

Dark brown curls fell across her face, her eyes widened. "Ay, ay, ay, Deputy...what's wrong? There's blood all over your face!"

"Let me in and lock the door, quickly."

Lupe peeked past Tempe before slamming the door and locking it. She turned on the lights and stared at Tempe. "There's blood everywhere! What happened to you?"

"Someone bashed me over the head." Tempe's knees gave way and she sank onto the couch, keeping her head forward to avoid dripping blood on the cushions.

"Who would do such an awful thing?" Lupe ran to the kitchen and ran water.

"I haven't the faintest idea," Tempe said.

"Where were you?" Lupe began dabbing at the wound with a wet dish cloth.

"Near the meadow."

"What were you doing there?"

"Coming to see you."

"Why?"

"Because you left a message for me to come here."

Lupe paused in her ministering. "No, I didn't."

"Blair told me you called. Said you wanted me to meet you here at midnight."

"I didn't call, Deputy Crabtree."

"But why would Blair make up such a thing?" Her head hurt so badly she couldn't think clearly.

"I don't know. I just know it wasn't me that called."

"Blair said you sounded funny, whispering like you were afraid someone might hear."

"Somebody must've pretended to be me. But why would anyone do that?"

"To bring me out here late at night so they could attack me when no one was around."

"But why?"

"To keep me from continuing my investigation into Andre Donato's death. Someone who knows Two John didn't do it and doesn't want me to find out who is guilty."

"If it hadn't been for your braid you'd probably be dead," Lupe said.

Touching the looped braid fastened with a large barrette to the back of her head, Tempe said, "Killing me was the goal, I'm sure." The wound was just above the top of the braid. Lupe was right, her thick hair had softened the blow.

"You probably ought to go into the hospital and have this checked. I bet you need stitches. You could have a concussion."

"I'll get it looked at as soon as I have time...but right now I better call into the sub-station and let them know what happened." Tempe automatically reached for her radio before remembering that both it and her gun had been stolen.

"That bump on the head must have affected me more than I realized. Whoever did this took my radio and my gun. I should have made my call as soon as I arrived. Can I use the phone?"

"Of course," Lupe said. She stepped inside what Tempe presumed was the bedroom and returned with a telephone on a long cord.

Tempe quickly punched the number for the sub-station before putting the instrument to her ear. Nothing happened. She depressed the button, there was no dial tone. "It's not working."

"I talked to my mother just before I went to bed. It was okay then."

Perhaps whoever waylaid Tempe had also cut the telephone line into Lupe's house, but Tempe didn't want to worry the young woman unnecessarily. "Probably something wrong with the lines." The phone system in Bear Creek often had problems.

"What're you going to do?" Lupe asked.

"I think it will be safer for both of us if I stay here until morning, if that's okay with you."

"Sure. I'll get you a blanket and pillow, though I don't think you ought to go to sleep just in case you do have a concussion."

"I don't think I could fall asleep even if I wanted to." Though Lupe had successfully stopped the bleeding, Tempe's head still throbbed painfully.

After bringing the bedding, Lupe asked, "What about some aspirin for your head? And something to drink, a soda or juice, maybe?"

"Probably be better if I didn't take any aspirin yet...might make me sleepy. But I could use some coffee.

"Instant, okay?" While busying herself in the kitchen, Lupe asked, "I can't imagine who would have attacked you like that."

"The only one I'm positive didn't do it, is Nick Two John. He's locked away in jail. Besides, I suppose it must have been a woman, since Blair thought it was you who called. Maybe it was Claudia, she's certainly been unhappy with me lately. She blames me for Nick being arrested. I really thought we had worked things out this evening...but she might have been even angrier than I thought and merely pretended to accept my explanation."

"Hitting you over the head doesn't really seem like something Mrs. Donato would do, does it?" The tea kettle whistled and Lupe poured the water into a mug which she brought to Tempe.

"Maybe it wasn't a woman who called," Lupe suggested as she put the cup down on the trunk that served as a coffee table.

"Surely Blair could have told the difference between a man's and a woman's voice."

"Didn't you say that the person whispered? I don't think you can really recognize a whisper."

Lupe was right. Tempe nodded, and she thought about it. The only men she'd talked to about the murder earlier were Edgar Van Tassel and Wilbur Carmony. Neither one had given her any reason to suspect impending violence. Though Van Tassel hadn't appreciated her questions, he'd neither said or done anything suspicious.

Wilbur going to see his wife right after being questioned could be considered suspicious—especially since Elise didn't stay at the inn to meet with Tempe as she'd promised. "Lupe, think back to when Mr. Donato was still alive. Tell me everything you can remember about how he acted with Elise Carmony."

"I already told you she had a big crush on Mr. Donato."

"Tell me everything you noticed about her and Mr. Donato. What made you think she had a crush on him? How did she act around him?"

Lupe pulled the wicker chair around in front of Tempe and

plopped down in it, tucking her flowered nightgown around her crossed legs. "I always thought she was kind of silly. She fluttered around him whenever he came into the kitchen, asking if she could fix him this or that. That's how she got started making him that special tea."

"Did he respond to her from the beginning?"

"Of course. He flirted with all females. He flattered us outrageously...especially Mrs. Carmony. Always told her how nice she looked...whether she did or not. None of the rest of us paid any attention to his nonsense, but Mrs. Carmony loved it. Pretty soon she started fixing herself up...wearing make-up and nice clothes, even dyed her hair."

"I noticed."

"So did Mr. Donato. I think he was impressed that she'd done all that special for him and he began getting cozy with her."

"What do you mean by 'getting cozy'?"

"Whenever he talked to her, he got really close. Always putting his arm around her, cuddling her, sliding his hand down her bottom...stuff like that. Caught them kissing once when I came to work a few minutes early."

"You told me before that you thought they'd been intimate...what gave you that idea?"

"Nothing in particular...it was just that Mrs. Carmony began acting even goonier whenever Mr. Donato came into the room. She'd bat her eyelashes, pet his arm or hand, and you know, kind of wiggle around him." Lupe stretched and yawned.

"And how did Mr. Donato respond?"

"At first, he seemed to enjoy it. If Mrs. Donato was gone, he'd have some reason for Mrs. Carmony to go into the office with him. And for awhile, Mrs. Carmony always sent us home while she stayed in the kitchen...supposedly to finish up."

"You said at first...when did things change?"

"A week or two before he died...maybe sooner. It happened gradual like. He just didn't come into the kitchen as often as he used to, and when he did, he didn't pay any special attention to Mrs. Carmony."

"How did this affect her?"

"She was still real nice to him, but she turned mean to the rest of us. One of the cooks said he wished she'd find a new boy friend." Lupe quickly covered her mouth as she yawned again.

"Why don't you go back to bed? I'll be fine."

A twig snapped outside. Tempe turned her head to listen. Something banged against the front door, followed by a repeated pounding.

Lupe screamed. Tempe's hand dropped to her empty holster.

Chapter 20

"QUIET, LUPE." Tempe leaped to her feet—a big mistake. Her head spun and she swayed, almost losing her balance.

Lupe bounded from her chair and grabbed Tempe's arm. "What is it?"

Tempe shook her head. She had no idea. Freeing herself from Lupe's grasp, Tempe made her way carefully to the door and pressed her ear against it. She could hear muffled sounds on the porch.

Without a weapon and still woozy from the blow to her head, she didn't think it wise to open the door and confront whoever or whatever was out there.

"Maybe it's a bear," Lupe whispered. She stood as close to Tempe as possible without touching her. "Sometimes bears tip over the garbage cans."

Tempe wished it were a bear on the porch, but the sounds they heard hadn't been made by an animal. Though she didn't know the identity of the person, she was positive whoever was outside was also responsible for the attack on her. "Lupe, have you got anything we can use to protect ourselves?"

"What about a baseball bat? I have one in my bedroom."

"Perfect," Tempe said, though she'd hoped for a shotgun or a rifle.

While Lupe went for the bat, Tempe listened through the door. She could hear someone going down the porch stairs and what she thought were stealthy footsteps around the cabin. But because the wind muffled the sound she couldn't even guess what was happening outside.

Lupe held the bat out to Tempe.

"I think you better hang onto that. I'm going to open the door fast. If there's anyone out there, don't hesitate to use that thing." Tempe carefully undid the chain so it wouldn't make any noise. No need to alert whoever was outside. She twisted the other lock and yanked on the door. It didn't move.

Gathering all of her strength, she pulled again. Nothing.

"Let me try." Lupe handed the bat to Tempe. She put both hands on the knob, turned and jerked. The door wouldn't budge. "What's the matter? Why won't it open?"

"It's been jammed...nailed shut, maybe. That must have been the pounding we heard. Where's your back door?"

Lupe looked stricken. "There isn't one."

"What?"

"These cabins are so little I guess they figured a back door wasn't necessary."

"We'll have to go out through there." As she started toward the only window in the living room, an explosion rocked the cabin sending Tempe and Lupe reeling backwards. Lupe screamed.

Flames licked at the front window. "Come on, we've got to get out of here." Tempe whirled around. Ominous black smoke poured in the open kitchen window.

Her head ached so much it was hard to think. "Damn, the whole place has been torched."

Lupe cried, "I'm so scared. Are we going to burn to death?"

Tempe jerked open the bathroom door. The tiny room held a toilet, sink, and shower and had a small, high window. "Bring that blanket off the couch." Tempe shoved aside the shower curtain and turned the cold water on full.

Grabbing the towels from the rack, Tempe threw them on the floor of the shower. With tears streaming down her face, Lupe thrust the blanket toward Tempe.

"Toss it in the shower. We want it as wet as we can get it."

"What're we going to do, Tempe?" Lupe wailed.

"We're going out through that window. With any luck, whoever did this is long gone."

Tempe shoved the window open, and coughed as smoke poured in. "Grab the blanket and wrap it around you. Climb up on the toilet and jump out as far as you can."

"What about you?"

"Don't worry, I'll be right behind you."

The bathroom window was shoulder high. Lupe pulled the dripping blanket around her like a shroud, stepped up onto the toilet seat and scrambled through the opening.

Tempe could hear a thud as the young woman hit the ground but she couldn't see anything because of the flames licking up the side of the building and the thick, black smoke. She scooped up the dripping towels and wrapped one around her head and face and tossed the other over her shoulders.

She pulled herself onto the toilet. Flames flared up from the window sill. Taking the towel from her shoulders she beat them out before wiggling through the narrow window. Striking the ground hard with her shoulder, the pain in her head intensified to the point she lost consciousness momentarily.

Hands tugged at her. "Tempe, Tempe. Oh, please be all right." Lupe dragged her a few feet from the fully engulfed cabin. Flames brightened the night and their crackling muffled all other sounds.

With Lupe's help, Tempe scrambled to her feet and staggered to another cabin.

"Who lives here?"

Still wrapped in the blanket with only her frightened face and bare feet exposed, Lupe said, "Nick Two John."

"Does he have a phone?"

"I suppose." Lupe looked puzzled.

Tempe tried the door, it was locked. Stove length logs had been stacked neatly on the porch. She picked up a thick piece and smashed it against the window. Reaching through the broken glass, she unlocked the door.

While looking for the phone by the flickering glow from the fire, her first scan of the room didn't reveal a telephone. If the fire department wasn't notified quickly, Nick's place would be ignited and probably the surrounding woods. Tempe hurried across a colorful woven rug with Indian designs, and past the wooden couch and chair upholstered in brown and white cowhide.

Remembering Lupe's phone had been in the bedroom, Tempe guessed perhaps the jack was in the same place in this cabin. She dashed into the other room and was rewarded by the sight of an old-fashioned rotary phone on a barrel table beside a simple bed. When she picked up the receiver, she sighed with relief at the sound of a steady tone. She quickly dialed 911.

"What is the nature of your emergency?" the dispatcher asked.

"This is Deputy Crabtree. I'm reporting a fire in one of the cabins behind Bear Creek Inn."

"Someone's already reported it, Deputy."

"Good." She replaced the receiver. Sirens wailed in the distance.

"Help is on the way," Tempe said when she rejoined Lupe outside. The young woman's cabin burned ferociously, the wind sending sparks flying. Because the cabins were located in the middle of cleared land, most of the live ash and sparks landed on dry ground and went out. "I'm not sure it's such a good idea for us to stand around out in the open like this."

Lupe's black eyes registered fear. "What do you mean? Do you think we're in danger from the fire?"

"Not yet, but that's a possibility. I'm more worried that whoever did this might still be lurking about. Why don't we go wait in the woods where we aren't such obvious targets?" Tempe took hold of Lupe's arm, not just to lead the girl to a safe refuge, but also to steady herself. The throbbing pain reminded her of her injury.

"Surely you don't think..." Lupe gasped as they darted toward a thick growth of cedars.

"I don't know what to think. If whoever did this is using his head, he's likely disappeared. But on the other hand, I can't imagine that whoever is responsible is thinking clearly. Setting a fire like this in the middle of the woods could be a disaster for the whole town of Bear Creek."

Tempe knew the only way for the fire engines to get into the area was on a crude road cut through the backside of the property. She expected some volunteer fire fighters to be arriving on foot soon. The quickest way to the fire was the path from the Inn's parking lot. Perhaps one of them would spot the guilty party.

Obviously believing the threat of harm still present, Lupe shrank back into the shadows of the tree trunks. Tempe had other plans. "Stay put until you see the volunteers," she warned.

"Where are you going?" Lupe asked, fearfully.

"I'm going to see if I can't catch up with whoever set the fire." Tempe didn't wait for an argument. Trying to ignore the pulsating pain in her head, she skirted the edge of the clearing. When she reached the place where the path toward the Inn began, instead of taking it, she made her way alongside, stepping around trees and bushes. The bright glow from the fire lit her way.

As she neared the spot where she'd been struck over the head, she slowed her pace. The fire still reddened the sky but no longer brightened the area. She circled around, searching for a clue of any kind—a snapped twig, a footprint.

When she'd about given up, a movement caught her eye. Something fluttered from a thorn of a crooked Manzanita branch. Tempe stepped closer. It was a scrap of cloth, dark blue with a white flower print.

She plucked the material from the thorn and dropped it into her pocket. Tempe knew who killed Andre Donato and tried to kill her.

The sound of galloping footsteps caught her attention and she stepped onto the path just as fire-fighters in turn-out gear and carrying shovels, rounded the bend.

"My Lord, Tempe, what on earth happened to you?" Charlene Goodsen gasped, pausing as she took in Tempe's bloodied head and soiled and sooty uniform.

"I'll tell you all about it later. The fire needs your attention now," Tempe said.

Charlene gave Tempe one last glance before falling in behind the man who'd gone on ahead.

Edgar Van Tassel, also outfitted in fire gear, loped toward her. "How bad is it, Crabtree?" He asked before he noted her disheveled condition. Halting, he frowned. "What's going on?"

"I had a little accident." Tempe decided to return to the fire. She might be able to help.

By the time they all reached the clearing, a fire truck and a water tender had arrived. Other helmeted and yellow- coated firemen were hauling hoses from the tender toward the fire. Chief Roundtree hollered out orders. Water sprays were aimed at the flames while the other volunteer crew used shovels to throw dirt on the small fires that had flared up in the underbrush around the perimeter.

Tempe spotted Lupe who'd come out of her hiding place.
With no emotions visible on her face, the young woman watched her home and all her belongings being consumed. She probably felt happy to be alive.

Other Bear Creek residents trickled down the path and stepped out into the clearing. The second wave of arrivals had come out of curiosity. A big fire always drew a crowd, no matter the time of day or night.

Claudia, wearing sandals and a silk wrapper the same color as the flames, called out to Tempe. "Where's Lupe, is she all right?"

"She's fine, see, there she is." Tempe pointed toward the girl.

"Anyone know how the fire got started?" Claudia looked at Tempe and her eyes grew big. "Tempe, what on earth happened to you? You're all bloody." Stepping behind her, Claudia took hold of Tempe's shoulders. "Oh, my God! That's terrible looking! You need to go to the hospital!"

"I can't yet. I've got some unfinished business."

"Nothing could possibly be more important than getting your head taken care of...I'm sure you need stitches."

Lupe spotted them, a huge smile brightening her face. She

discarded the blanket and ran to Tempe and Claudia. "Mrs. Donato, did Deputy Crabtree tell you? Someone tried to kill us! Tempe saved my life!"

"What's this? You better tell me what's been going on." Claudia frowned at Tempe.

"It's a long story. Lupe can tell you. I'd appreciate it if you'd take care of her for me. Obviously she has no where to stay now."

Claudia draped an arm around the young woman's shoulder. "Don't worry about her, she can stay at the inn. But I want to know..."

"Not now," Tempe said, as she spotted Elise Carmony partly hidden behind several Bear Creek residents. The woman's protruding eyes were fixed on the firemen's efforts to put out the flames. A strange smile partially lifted the corners of her lips.

Without losing sight of the woman, Tempe edged her way through the crowd, ignoring those who attempted talking to her. Elise didn't notice Tempe, she was too enraptured by the fire.

Coming up behind her, Tempe noticed Elise was still wearing the dark blue apron with the white flower print...a corner had been ripped away.

"Elise," Tempe said.

The woman whirled around, her face contorted into a ghastly mask. "You! You're supposed to be dead!"

A smell of gasoline wafted from Elise like strong perfume as she pulled Tempe's revolver from her pocket. "You won't get away from me this time!"

Chapter 21

NEARBY, A woman screamed. The wound in Tempe's head pounded. Elise raised Tempe's gun.

A man shouted, "Look out, she's going to shoot."

Adrenalin charged, Tempe grabbed Elise's arm and forced the revolver toward the ground. The gun fired. The screaming became louder. Still yanking on Elise's arm, Tempe shoved hard, knocking her off balance. She landed with a thud and Tempe fell on top of her.

While Elise was momentarily disoriented, Tempe snatched the gun from her hand and rolled away and into a sitting position.

Elise started to get up, but Tempe scrambled to her feet, holding the gun with both hands, she aimed it at her.

"Stay right where you are! You're under arrest for the murder of Andre Donato and the attempted murder of Lupe Madrid. You have the right to remain silent..." Tempe recited the rest of the rights to the background of the crowd's curious questioning and the shouts of the firemen and volunteers.

When she'd finished, Tempe asked, "Did you understand what I said, Elise?"

"Yes, of course I understood," Elise snapped.

Pete Roundtree appeared beside Tempe. He pulled off his helmet revealing his straight black hair. Scratching behind one of his slightly protruding ears he stared at her. "Anything I can help you with, Deputy?"

"There certainly is. I don't have my radio. Please, call the dispatcher for me. Ask for a deputy to be sent up here to take in Mr. Donato's murderer. By the way, Mrs. Carmony is also responsible for the fire."

A lifted eyebrow was all that displayed his surprise at Tempe's announcement. "Okay. Anything else? You don't look so good."

"I don't feel so good." Tempe holstered her gun and reached for her handcuffs. "Take hold of Mrs. Carmony while I cuff her."

With her hands fastened behind her, Mrs. Carmony mumbled, "He deserved to die."

"Pete, get me a deputy up here right away."

Roundtree nodded and hurried away in the direction of his fire engine.

Tempe led Elise to a fallen log. "Sit down and relax. It'll be awhile."

"Any woman in my place would have done the same."

"Remember, Elise, you don't have to say anything." Tempe dropped down beside her.

The firemen continued to saturate the blackened shell of the cabin with water. Smoke and ash clogged the night air.

The crowd circled around Tempe and Elise, but Elise seemed unaware of anyone but Tempe. "I thought he loved me. I would have done anything he wanted. But I meant nothing to him, he didn't care for me at all. It hurt so bad and he acted like nothing had happened between us. I couldn't let him get away with it."

Because of all the curious faces, Tempe again tried to halt Elise's confession. "This isn't the right time for..."

"It doesn't matter. Nothing matters anymore. No one should have ever known what killed Andre. Natural causes, that's what it should have been called." Elise's eyes stared past the folks crowding close to her.

Since it was obvious she couldn't stop Elise, Tempe decided to clear up some of her own questions. "What made you decide to use the Lily of the Valley to kill Andre?"

"Went on one of Two John's foolish nature walks. Asked him enough questions to know exactly how to get back at Andre for humiliating me the way he did." Elise squirmed on the log as though trying to make herself more comfortable.

"It was so easy. I picked up a couple of the vases with the lilies, and dumped the water into the pitcher I used to make Andre's special tea. With all the herbs I used, he never even noticed any difference in the taste." Her smile was mirthless. "He even refilled his glass a couple of times. I'm just sorry he didn't suffer more...like he made me suffer."

Some of the listeners gasped, but Elise didn't seem to notice. She lifted her head toward Tempe, a sneer distorting her mouth. "You didn't have any idea I was responsible."

"That's not quite true, Elise. At first I didn't suspect you. But tonight I've been thinking about how you acted when Andre died. You seemed to grieve too much. Yet you weren't very surprised to learn what killed him. When your husband told me what had really been going on with you and Andre, I began considering you as a suspect. He said you didn't have an affair with Andre...and he was right. Andre didn't care about you at all.

"I really began to wonder when you disappeared after promising to meet me with me."

Elise's lips drew back from her teeth in what might have been an attempt at a smile. "Of course. My stupid husband told me what he said to you. Obviously it was only a matter of time until you'd be badgering me about what part I had in Andre's death. I knew I had to get rid of you."

"You called my house and told my son you were Lupe."

"That's right. Worked too, didn't it? All I had to do was wait until Wilbur drank himself into a stupor like he does every night. I took a hammer and hid out alongside the trail. You didn't have any idea you were in danger when you came along there. It was simple to leap out and smash you with that hammer. I hit you hard enough to kill you. Thought I had. Threw away your radio and took your gun just in case."

"What made you come back to check?" Tempe asked. Her head was really throbbing again.

"I don't know. I was already in my car when I had this feeling. Opened my trunk and found a case of pop bottles and a can of gasoline and knew exactly what I had to do. Stopped off in the kitchen and picked up a tea towel, a box of matches, and some nails. Sure enough, when I got to the spot on the trail you were gone. Lupe's was the only place you could be.

"I spotted the both of you through the window. Filled one of the bottles with gasoline and stuffed the tea towel in it. Nailed the door shut, lit the tea towel and threw the bottle onto the porch. It worked beautifully. I splashed gasoline all around the house. Fire started everywhere. I didn't expect you to be able to get out of there. Unfortunately, I was wrong."

"Mom!" Blair, his blond hair bright above the crowd, elbowed his way toward Tempe. "Are you all right?"

Hutch was right behind Blair. Worry pleated his brow as he grasped her shoulders and took in her bloodstained uniform and uncombed hair. "Dear God in Heaven, what's happened to you?" He pulled her close.

"What's going on, Mom?" Blair asked, glancing toward Elise who sat slumped on the log, arms behind her.

Tempe ignored their questions. "What are you doing here?"

"Your dispatcher couldn't raise you on the radio so she called the house. She told me about the fire and your request for back-up.

Thought I better see what was going on."

"And thank God he had the presence of mind to call me," Hutch said. "Where did all that blood come from?"

"Elise hit me with a hammer."

"What?" He glared at the woman. "Why did she do that? Let me see."

Tempe tipped her head forward. "She killed Andre, and she wanted to kill me because she knew I would be after her."

"Oh, sweetheart, that looks really bad. Has anyone looked at it?"

"Lots of folks. And everyone agrees with you, that it looks bad. It doesn't feel so good either."

"You probably need stitches. Let me take you to the doctor," Hutch said.

"Yeah, Mom."

"I can't go anywhere yet," Tempe said. "I have to wait until a deputy arrives to take Mrs. Carmony to jail."

"But what if you have a concussion, or you're in shock or something?" Blair asked.

"I feel a lot better than I did awhile ago. If I were going to drop dead from this wound I think it would have happened by now. Besides, there's nothing I can do but stand by until I get a replacement."

Because the firemen had doused most of the flames, it was getting darker and darker. The lights from the emergency vehicles cutting through the thick smoke cast an eerie red and yellow pallor over everything.

"Hey, Crabtree, what you got here?" Deputy Bradley appeared through the haze. "Who's this killer you want brought it? Why can't you do it?" The young deputy's handsome face puckered as he came close enough to notice Tempe's bloodied and disheveled appearance.

Tempe pointed at Elise sitting on the log. "I've arrested Elise Carmony for Andre Donato's murder, and for the attempted murder of Lupe Madrid."

Blair put in quickly, "She tried to kill my mother too."

"Wow!" the Deputy said. "You got the evidence to prove everything?"

"All these people standing around here heard her confession," Tempe said.

"That's right, Deputy," a voice said, with several more agreeing.

"Take her apron and put it into an evidence bag," Tempe said. "It reeks of the gasoline she used to set fire to the cabin, and it has a torn place that matches this."

From her pocket Tempe fished out the scrap of material she'd discovered caught on the manzanita branch. "I found this close by where I was attacked. And I think if you search her car you'll find a six-pack of empties with one bottle missing, and possibly the hammer that she used to hit me over the head with."

"What about your report?" Bradley asked.

"I'll have to take care of it tomorrow." Tempe felt weak and her legs gave way. She would have fallen if Hutch hadn't caught her.

His voice sounded as if it came from faraway though she could feel his strong arms around her, supporting her, cradling her. "That's it. I'm taking you to the doctor right now."

Though Tempe felt like she ought to argue...there was so much more she needed to do...Sergeant Guthrie had to be called so Two John could be freed. A warm blackness closed in around her. The last thing she remembered was Hutch scooping her into his arms.

A STABBING PAIN to the back of her head awakened Tempe. She found herself lying on her side on a narrow examining table. When she tried to raise her head, she was restrained by a heavy hand.

She recognized Dr. McClatchey's voice as he said, "Lie still, Deputy. I'm going to stitch this nasty wound as soon as the anesthetic takes effect."

"Anesthetic...I don't want to be knocked out again!"

"Don't worry, it's only a local."

She knew she was in the small office in Dr. McClatchey's home. "Where are Hutch and Blair?"

"In the kitchen with my wife. She's making some coffee. Though they both wanted to stay with you, I didn't think either one of them were up to watching me sew you up. I'm not fond of scooping the squeamish off the floor." He chuckled. "I understand you've had an exciting night."

"You could say that. How bad is it, Doctor?"

"Not as bad as it looks. A few stitches will take care of the wound. I don't think there's any need for you to go to the hospital if you'll take it easy for awhile. If you're as hard headed as I suspect, you ought to be able to go back to work in a couple of days."

"There are some things I need to take care of..." Tempe began.

"Someone else can do it for you. You're mighty fortunate, young lady. I could be doing an autopsy instead of patching you up."

Tempe realized the truth of his statement. If Elise had done what she'd meant to, Tempe would be dead. All she wanted to do was put everything else out of her mind except her love for Hutch and her son.

After Dr. McClatchey finished, he escorted her into the large kitchen. Mrs. McClatchey in night clothes, her short white hair uncombed, sat at one end of an oval, golden oak table. Hutch and Blair sat opposite her. In front of each one was a steaming mug on a green quilted place mat. Tempe could smell the freshly brewed coffee.

Mrs. McClatchey was the first to notice her husband and his patient. Her tanned and wrinkled face showed concern as she said, "Oh, my dear, do come sit down."

"Tempe, sweetheart, let me help you." Hutch leaped to his feet and ran to her side. Blair pulled out a chair. With his arm around her, Hutch guided her into it.

"Hey, Mom, how're you doing?"

Tempe shrugged as she settled into the seat. "Not bad."

Mrs. McClatchey put a full mug of coffee on the mat in front of her. "Would you like sugar or cream, my dear?"

"No, thank you."

After pouring his own coffee, Dr. McClatchey leaned against the polished oak cupboards. "It isn't necessary for Tempe to go to the hospital. But I'm putting you both in charge of seeing that she rests for a couple of days."

"That's not going to be easy," Hutch said.

"I have to use the phone," Tempe said.

"See what I mean?" Hutch said. "Who do you want to call?"

"I have to tell the Sergeant to give the order to release Two John."

Hutch grinned. "I already took care of it. Nick should soon be on his way back to Bear Creek. Though I must say, Sergeant Guthrie isn't the most personable of souls."

Being awakened before dawn wouldn't have helped the Sergeant's disposition, nor would have finding out that Tempe had disobeyed his order and continued her own investigation of Donato's murder. She hoped he'd forgiven her after hearing she'd arrested the real murderer. And the fact that Hutch made the call surely meant he'd gotten over his jealousy of Two John.

"When are you getting married?" Mrs. McClatchey asked.

"Real soon now, thank God," Hutch answered quickly.

Tempe squeezed his hand.

Blair beamed. "I've been waiting for this for a long time."

"Have you decided where you will live?" the doctor asked. "I know you own that nice ranch, Pastor, and Tempe has her cottage down the road."

"We haven't made up our..." Tempe began.

Hutch interrupted, "I'm thinking of selling the ranch. Someone made me a great offer."

"Oh, Hutch. Is that what you really want? I know your family has owned that place for years."

"Frankly I'll be happy to be rid of it. It's too much work. We can have a nice savings to begin married life with. We might even build onto your house, if you'd like." Hutch put his arm around her.

Blair beamed at them both.

Tempe no longer noticed the pain in her head. It was only a matter of days before she'd become Hutch's wife.

~ * ~

Marilyn Meredith

Marilyn Meredith has been writing professionally for more than twenty-five years. She's written for local newspapers and national magazines, and has published many how-to books and monthly newsletters for the community care industry. As a means to tell people about writing and electronic publishing, and for promotion, Marilyn has spoken at various writers' conferences, schools, and for service clubs. She's had two historical family sagas based on her own family genealogy published, as well as a mystery with supernatural twist called THE ASTRAL GIFT.

Marilyn is a member of Sisters in Crime, Mystery Writers of America, Novelists Inc., California Writers Club, and EPIC. Besides teaching weekly writing class, she is also an instructor for Writer's Digest Schools.

Married for over forty years to the sailor she met on a blind date, Marilyn is the mother of five grown children, eighteen grandchildren and six great-grandchildren.

Writing is Marilyn's greatest escape. She says there is nothing more gratifying than going into a world where she is in control--or at least thinks she is.

Visit Marilyn's web site at:

Don't miss…

Deadly Omen

Book 1 in the Tempe Crabtree Mystery Series

A CANDIDATE for Princess is murdered at a Native American Pow Wow while Tempe is working there in her capacity as deputy. Tempe's investigation takes her into the Yanduchi reservation, and Hutch has difficulty with Tempe's growing interest in her own native heritage as she seeks the identity of the killer.

Penny Warner, *author of the* **Connor Westphal series** *has this to say about Deadly Omen:*

"Deputy Crabtree is proud of her mixed-Indian heritage and enjoys working among the people of Bear Creek, California. When she's assigned to keep watch over a Pow Wow celebration she's drawn into the death of a beautiful Pow Wow Princess. A feather left behind is Tempe's only clue. Set against the drumbeats and dances of the festivities, Deadly Omen builds to an exciting climax, as the reader absorbs the color and culture of this unique mountain community."

Coming in ebook January 2002
from
Hard Shell Word Factory
www.hardshell.com